"You Are Really Spoiled!"

she said. "You're so used to private pools and private clubs and—"

His hand at the nape of her neck silenced the spate of words. Logan pulled her closer, brushed his lips over her cheek, murmuring in her ear, "You know why I don't want anyone else around."

Lisa felt the silken web of danger enfolding her. The thing she wanted most in the world was to melt against him.

With a tremendous effort, she looked away from the flame in those blue eyes.

"I think you've had too much sun," she said unsteadily.

TRACY SINCLAIR
has worked extensively as a photo journalist. She's traveled throughout North America, as well as parts of the Caribbean, South America and Europe. Her name is very familiar in both Silhouette Romances and Silhouette Special Editions.

Dear Reader:

I'd like to take this opportunity to thank you for all your support and encouragement of Silhouette Romances.

Many of you write in regularly, telling us what you like best about Silhouette, which authors are your favorites. This is a tremendous help to us as we strive to publish the best contemporary romances possible.

All the romances from Silhouette Books are for you, so enjoy this book and the many stories to come. I hope you'll continue to share your thoughts with us, and invite you to write to us at the address below:

Karen Solem
Editor-in-Chief
Silhouette Books
P.O. Box 769
New York, N.Y. 10019

TRACY SINCLAIR
Stars in Her Eyes

Silhouette Romance

Published by Silhouette Books New York

America's Publisher of Contemporary Romance

SILHOUETTE BOOKS, a division of Simon & Schuster, Inc.
1230 Avenue of the Americas, New York, N.Y. 10020

ISBN: 0-671-57244-X

First Silhouette Books printing September, 1983

10 9 8 7 6 5 4 3 2 1

Map by Ray Lundgren

America's Publisher of Contemporary Romance

Printed in the U.S.A.
BC91

Other Silhouette Books by Tracy Sinclair

Paradise Island
Holiday in Jamaica
Never Give Your Heart
Mixed Blessing
Flight to Romance
Designed for Love
Castles in the Air
Fair Exchange

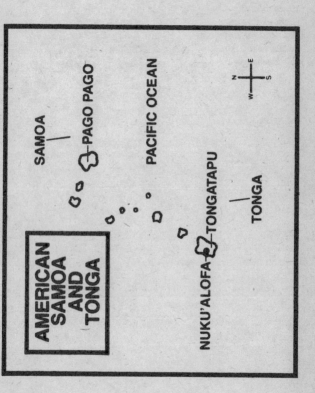

Stars in Her Eyes

Chapter One

The windshield wipers on the small Morris Minor waged a losing battle with the torrential rain. November was the wet season in Los Angeles but it seldom stormed like this, which was small comfort to Lisa Brooks. Gripping the wheel tightly, she peered through the streaming windshield as the little car skittered around the sharp curves of Coldwater Canyon.

Rocks and mud slides were encroaching on the road and to add to her troubles, the Morris was making warning noises again. *Oh please, dear Lord, not tonight,* she begged!

The car was four years old when she bought it and had worked reasonably well for a time but it wasn't made to take the hills. When Lisa signed up for a night course in the San Fernando Valley, a suburb over the hills from Los Angeles where she lived, the little car began to protest vigorously. It had broken down with a regularity that was becoming monotonous, forcing her to beg the use of a phone from houses on both sides of the mountain. But this night was the worst.

For one thing, it was eleven P.M., and who was going to answer the door at that hour? For another thing, she was approaching the summit where there were only huge mansions set well back from the road.

It would really have been wiser to skip class, feeling the way she did, but there was a guest speaker that Lisa especially wanted to hear. For all the good she got out of it though, she might as well have stayed home. The cold she caught a week before had worsened, making her feel alternately burning hot and freezing cold.

When the car chugged over the summit and died with a racking cough that coincided with one of her own, Lisa felt like bursting into tears. Here she was in the middle of the wilderness and what was she going to do now?

It was a great temptation to go completely to pieces but, taking herself firmly in hand, she wiped a clear spot on the steamy windshield and saw a pair of stately stone gates guarding a long curving driveway. A glimmer of lights in the distance indicated a house and, grimly, Lisa got out of the car. If they wouldn't let her in, maybe they would at least call the auto club for her. Those stalwart gentlemen had gotten to be her best friends.

The driveway was dark and spooky and seemed to wind on forever. It was lined with dense shrubbery and towering trees that appeared to be alive. When the first branches reached out for her like clutching hands, Lisa uttered a small yelp of fear, but after a while numbness set in. Nothing really mattered anymore because she felt like she was floating several feet above the ground.

Through the rain that soaked her to the skin, lights beckoned and receded like secret signals, guiding her to an imposing white house that looked like a fairy castle. Was this all just an hallucination?

Shaking her head to clear it, she pressed the bell. After a short interval, the door opened, revealing a tall man in a black suit who looked at her impassively. "I'm sorry to disturb you," she faltered, "but could I use your phone? My car has broken down."

"That is not very original, young lady," he said disapprovingly, the lines in his face deepening.

"I beg your pardon?" His voice seemed to come from a

great distance and Lisa wasn't sure she had heard him correctly.

"Couldn't you have tried a more innovative approach?" he asked contemptuously.

The door was starting to close and she panicked. "Please help me! You don't have to let me in. If you'll just call the auto club, I'll be eternally grateful!"

"You can use the phone at the gas station. It's at the bottom of the hill," the man said with finality.

A cold wind lifted the skirts of Lisa's raincoat, the darkness seeming to clutch at her with avid fingers. Only the narrowing slice of golden light promised salvation and she pushed against the door desperately. "You can't turn me away! All I'm asking for is a phone call."

"Who is it, Rogers?" A deep male voice caused the man to look over his shoulder.

"It's another of those would-be actresses, Mr. Marshall. Don't trouble yourself, I'll deal with it."

His words didn't even register but, hearing another voice, Lisa hoped she would find someone with a spark of humanity. Pushing her way inside, she cried, "My car is dead and there isn't another house on top of the hill. I'll wait outside but won't you please make a phone call for me?"

Her confused senses registered a huge entry hall with a graceful curving staircase facing the door. The carpeting was a thick, pale beige, and Lisa was miserably aware of the fact that she was dripping all over it. It wasn't calculated to endear her to the owner, she thought despairingly.

He moved toward her and she wasn't reassured. Although she was reasonably tall, he towered over her, his hawklike face wearing a frown. She had a swift impression of high cheekbones and dark hair falling over a broad, tanned forehead, but it was his piercing eyes that riveted her. They were an almost startling shade of blue.

As she gazed up at him beseechingly, another man appeared and asked, "What's up, Logan?"

"I'm not sure."

Lisa turned to the other man, who seemed more approachable. "All I want to do is use the phone." She had repeated the words so often she was beginning to sound like a robot, Lisa thought wildly.

"That doesn't seem unreasonable." He smiled.

"Maybe yes and maybe no," the first man grunted.

"Oh, come on, Logan, you're getting paranoid."

Lisa fumbled in her purse and took out her wallet. "Here's my card. Just tell them I'll be waiting in the car."

The man named Logan subjected her to an intense scrutiny before making up his mind. "Come into the den," he ordered brusquely.

Breathing a sigh of relief, Lisa followed him into a big room with book-lined walls and a glowing fireplace at one end, flanked by a long couch and comfortable chairs. A large desk with a telephone on it faced the door and she made for it gratefully.

She was so thoroughly chilled that her teeth were chattering as she asked, "Could I please borrow your phone book?"

"You'd better get out of those wet things and warm up by the fire first," the man she assumed to be the homeowner said. The words were considerate but his eyes were still cool.

"No, it's all right." A racking cough left her breathless but as soon as she could speak, Lisa said, "I'd better make my call."

"Do as I say. I'll pour you a brandy."

His manner was so autocratic that Lisa found herself following instructions, although she was beginning to be uneasy. It had been difficult to get in here, was it going to be equally difficult to get out? But she was shivering so uncontrollably that the fire was irresistible.

The hood of her raincoat had been pulled down to afford as much shelter as possible and when she pushed it back now and removed the shapeless garment, both men drew in their breath sharply.

"Sweet charity, what a face!" The second man whistled.

Lisa pushed the damp auburn hair off her forehead and looked at them out of frightened emerald eyes, blinking her wet, star-pointed lashes rapidly to clear her vision. The warm room, after the cold outside, was making everything dance around crazily.

"Who are you?" the man named Logan demanded, his gaze raking her slender, curved body.

She pulled her white sweater down nervously, regretting the gesture as his eyes moved to the upward tilt of her firm young breasts. "My . . . my name is Lisa Brooks."

"Do you know who I am?" he challenged.

She shook her head helplessly, looking at the other man for help.

Her instinct was correct because he said, "Allow me to introduce myself, since my friend's manners leave much to be desired. I'm Brian Metcalfe and this conquistador is Logan Marshall."

They both looked at her expectantly. "I . . . I'm very happy to meet both of you," she faltered, wondering what else she was supposed to say.

Logan was looking at her cynically. "I suppose you just happen to have a script in your pocket with a part you'd like to read for me."

It was like a scene out of *Alice in Wonderland*. What had she blundered into? Lisa had only been in Los Angeles for a little over two months, but even in her native Texas, there had been talk about the kinky people who inhabited Hollywood. Measuring the distance to the door, she began to inch toward it. "I think I'd better get back to my car now."

"Wait a minute." Logan started toward her. "What kind of game are you playing?"

The cruel twist of his sensual mouth frightened the daylights out of her and she started to run for the door, but he caught her effortlessly. His hands were firm on her shoulders and although she tried to struggle, her arms and legs felt like they were stuffed with cotton. From being freezing cold, she felt burning hot, and when the man named Brian put his hand on her cheek, she could only look at him with terrified eyes.

"Lie down on the couch," he said gently.

That galvanized her and she opened her mouth to scream but nothing came out. The room spun around and Lisa felt strong arms lifting her against a muscled chest. Then everything went dark.

"Put her on the sofa and tell Rogers to get my bag out of the car," Brian Metcalfe said crisply. "I think we have a very sick young lady here."

His hands were gentle as he touched her forehead, and a short time later used a stethoscope to listen to her labored breathing.

"Nothing like having a doctor for a best friend," Logan quipped, although his eyes were concerned. "Is she really as sick as she looks?"

"Worse. I think it's pneumonia. I'll have to get her to the hospital immediately."

He moved toward the phone but Logan stopped him. "You can't take her out in weather like this! There could be mud slides by now and even if the road is clear, you won't be able to go over fifteen miles an hour in this storm."

"I can't help it, I don't want to wait for an ambulance. She needs help, and fast!"

"Then bring it here," Logan said decisively. "Call for some nurses and any equipment you need. That will cut the time in half. I'll put her to bed upstairs."

"That might be a better idea at that. It's cold and nasty out." He paused with his hand on the phone, looking at his friend ironically. "Isn't this out of character for you? What's the matter, is your conscience hurting because you misjudged the poor girl?"

Logan scooped the inert Lisa into his arms and started out the door. "Get on with it and don't be such an idiot," he snapped impatiently.

Lisa was quiet in his arms as he carried her effortlessly up the wide staircase and into a large bedroom. But when he set her gently on the broad bed and moved to a bureau, she stirred restlessly, pulling at the neck of her sweater. "I'm hot . . . it's too warm," she mumbled.

He was at her side instantly, carefully pulling the sweater over her head and slipping off the navy wool skirt while she watched him uncomprehendingly out of fever-bright eyes. But when she was stripped to a lacy bra and brief silk panties, a shudder passed through her and the feathery brows drew together in a frown.

"I'm so cold," she whimpered, sliding her arms around his waist and cuddling close to him.

Logan's arms closed around her, and as he looked down at the delicate cheek nestled so trustingly on his shoulder, an expression crossed his face that would have surprised most of the people who knew him. It bore no resemblance to the wintry look they were used to seeing in those cold blue eyes.

After a moment's hesitation, he unclasped the wispy bra and reached for the silk pajama jacket he had brought from the bureau. But when the creamy, pink-tipped breasts were exposed, he paused. Accustomed as he was to female pulchritude, Logan caught his breath at the perfection of the slim body he held in his arms. It wasn't until Lisa stirred restlessly and tried to move close to him again that he quickly buttoned her into the pajama top and slid her between the covers.

"Okay, everything's set in motion," Brian said, coming into the room. "A nurse will be here within half an hour if we're lucky, and I've sent for a tank of oxygen just in case."

"Is she that badly off?"

"Well, you can see for yourself she's delirious. It's the high fever; we have to bring that down." He approached the bed and opened his bag. "Step aside, Logan."

The nurse arrived a short time later, and after conferring with her in low tones, Brian motioned to the other man. "Everything is under control here. We'd better go downstairs and see if we can find out anything about her."

Lisa's purse was lying where she dropped it but when Brian started going through it, Logan objected. "I don't feel right about this."

"I know what you mean, but right now all we know is her name. Somebody, someplace, is probably worried sick about her."

But the contents of the purse weren't that helpful. In addition to the usual lipstick, handkerchief and comb, all it contained was a small amount of money and a wallet with one bank card and a driver's license.

"It looks like she's a tourist," Brian commented. "Lisa Brooks, born 1959—that would make her twenty-four— address: 42 Poplar Place, Abilene, Texas. Well, at least nobody's frantic about her tonight. Tomorrow we can call her people and they can make arrangements about putting her in the hospital."

Logan frowned. "I don't see any point in moving her."

Brian ran a hand through his light brown hair, staring at the other man with raised eyebrows. Although they had been friends since college days, Logan still had the power to surprise him. "Isn't this quite a switch for you? You spend all your time trying to keep women out of here— except for selected ones of course." He smiled sardonically. "And now you want to saddle yourself with a little waif who faints on your doorstep."

"She's different—she needs help," Logan said stiffly.

"And what happens when she wakes up and discovers that by a great stroke of fortune she just happened to land in the lap of the famous Logan Marshall—the man who can make any girl into a star overnight?"

Logan scowled at his friend's mocking face. "Are you trying to tell me she's faking this illness?"

"No, of course not. I'm just trying to warn you that when she gets better—which I sincerely hope she will—" his face sobered for a moment "—she will probably be no different from all the other little starlets with their eyes out for the main chance."

"In that case, I'll turn her out." Logan shrugged.

Brian eyed his friend thoughtfully. "I wonder."

The nurse appeared in the doorway. "I think you should come, Dr. Metcalfe. She's very restless."

It was morning before Lisa's fever broke and Brian felt it was safe to leave. "I'm going home for a quick shower and then I have to go to the office, but I suggest you get some sleep," he told Logan.

"No, I have a conference this morning," Logan answered absently, looking down at a sleeping Lisa.

Both men were standing by the bed, talking in hushed tones. Her long eyelashes fluttered every now and then against pale cheeks but her breathing was even now.

"You should have gotten some sleep last night," Brian said disapprovingly. "It didn't take two of us to hold the vigil." Taking his friend by the arm, he led him out of the room. "I've arranged for nurses around the clock and everything is under control, so don't worry. Oh, and by the way, I'll try and get a phone number for that address in Texas."

"You needn't bother." Logan frowned. "I'll take care of it."

The next three days passed in a blur for Lisa. Most of the time she slept, awakening occasionally when a woman in a starched white uniform lifted her head to give her something to drink. A big friendly man with a soothing voice lived in her shadowy world too, putting things on her arm and taking her pulse.

But there was someone else. Often, she would awake to find a tall, dark man standing over her, his hands gentle as they smoothed the silky hair off her forehead. Or was she just imagining it? The way she imagined lying in his arms and being comforted by the reassuring strength of his hard, lean body?

One morning all the cobwebs were gone and Lisa sat up and looked around a completely unfamiliar room. She was lying in the middle of a large four-poster bed with a white eyelet tester on top. The fabric was duplicated in long billowing curtains at the windows and provided a fresh contrast to the dark blue carpet and blue velvet chaise.

A woman in a starched uniform got up from a chair. "Are you feeling better this morning?" She smiled.

Lisa stared at her in bewilderment. "Who are you? And where is this place?"

She started to throw back the covers but the woman urged her back onto the pillows. "Just lie back, my dear."

A thrill of apprehension ran through her. "No, I want to get up! Why are you trying to keep me here?"

"What's going on, Mrs. Dempster?" A man appeared in the doorway and Lisa clutched at the covers. It was the man in her misty dreams.

He had on a pair of gray flannels and there was a towel slung around his neck but his bronzed chest was bare, showing a mat of dark, curly hair that descended in a vee to his navel. Approaching the bed, he smiled down at her. The effect was dazzling, completely transforming the rather forbidding look he had worn on entering the room. "So you finally decided to come back and join us."

"Who are you?" she whispered.

"I'm Logan Marshall." He hesitated, but when that provoked no response, he asked, "Don't you remember?"

She shook her head. "Do I know you?"

He looked at her intently. "Your car broke down in the storm; you came to use the phone."

Her memory returned slowly. She looked at the bright sunshine streaming through the windows of the unfamiliar bedroom and a hint of panic lit her wide green eyes. "But that was last night. What am I doing in this room?"

"You've been very sick," he told her gravely. "You had us worried for a few days."

"A few *days!* How long have I been here?"

"Well, well, it looks like our patient has turned the corner." Brian came in the door and strode over to the other side of the bed, reaching for her wrist.

Lisa flinched away and huddled back against the pillows. "I don't know what's going on but I wish you would all go away so I can get dressed. I have to go to work."

The two men frowned at each other over her head and Logan said, "Is she still delirious?"

"I didn't think so, but it looks like it."

"Will you please stop talking about me as if I'm not here?" Lisa cried. "There is nothing wrong with me! I had a little cold but that was no excuse for putting me to bed." She pulled the covers up to her chin, a rosy blush highlighting her cheekbones as she added indignantly, "And it better have been that woman who undressed me!"

A slight smile tilted Logan's firm mouth as Brian said, "You had more than a little cold, young lady. You had pneumonia and it was touch and go there for a while."

"Really?" Her wide eyes searched their faces. "Well, I . . . I'm sorry if I was a nuisance but if you'll just leave me alone, I'd like to get dressed now and then I'll get out of your way."

"You aren't going anywhere," Brian told her sternly. "Didn't you hear what I told you?"

"But I'm fine now and I have to go to work. What time is it? I'm probably late already."

"What's all this about going to work?" Logan asked. "Aren't you just visiting here in Los Angeles? Your driver's license gave an address in Texas."

"That's where I used to live. I applied for a California license when I moved here two months ago and they told me I could use my old one until it came through."

Brian was regarding Logan steadily. "Didn't you try to contact her relatives in Abilene?"

"I didn't see any reason to disturb them until there was something positive to report," he replied austerely.

Brian turned disgustedly to Lisa. "If you'll give me your phone number in Texas, I'll contact anyone who might be worried about you."

She shook her head. "Thank you, but there isn't anyone."

He looked at her piercingly. "I can hardly believe that."

"It's the reason I came to California," she said simply. "My . . . my father died three months ago." Her eyes were bright with unshed tears and she blinked rapidly. "He was all the family I had and it was so . . . well, I just wanted to get away."

Brian patted her hand comfortingly. "I see. Well then, all you have to concentrate on is getting well." Turning to the nurse who was hovering discreetly in the background, he said, "I'll leave some instructions for you, Mrs. Dempster."

"Wait!" Lisa cried. Lowering her voice, she said, "Is she a private nurse?" When Brian nodded, her agitation increased. "How long has she been here?"

"Since the night you took ill. You're coming along fine now though," he reassured her. "We let the other nurses go."

"*Other* nurses!" She closed her eyes momentarily. "Good heavens, I can't afford that!"

"Why don't you let me worry about it?" Logan smiled down at her.

"And I can't stay here either," she told him.

"I'm afraid you're in no condition to go anywhere else," he said, with what looked strangely like satisfaction although Lisa knew it couldn't be.

"I know you don't want me here." She pushed up the long sleeves of the pajama coat, twisting her slim fingers together nervously. "Everything about that night is fuzzy but I do remember how angry you were that I rang your doorbell."

Ignoring Brian's sardonic look, Logan said evenly, "We'll talk about it when you're better."

"But I have to get up," she wailed. "I'll lose my job."

Brian took a hand. "You're going to stay right here and you're not going to upset yourself about anything or you'll have a relapse—and then you'll be here a lot longer. Do you understand me?" he asked sternly.

She nodded weakly, realizing for the first time how

exhausted she felt. The two men left her alone and she tried to concentrate on a solution to all the problems facing her but it seemed easier to drift off to sleep.

A large basket of red roses was the first thing Lisa saw when she opened her eyes in the late afternoon.

"Aren't they gorgeous?" Mrs. Dempster asked. "Mr. Marshall sent them. Such a nice, thoughtful man. It just shows you shouldn't go by anything you read in the paper." Lisa was puzzled but before she could ask for clarification, the nurse held out a beautiful lavender satin nightgown ornamented with lavish lace across the bosom. "Now that you're awake, how would you like to get out of that king-sized pajama coat? It's big enough for three little ones like you."

"Where did that come from?" Lisa eyed the nightgown.

"Mr. Marshall sent it along with the roses."

"I can't accept it!"

"Why ever not?"

A thought occurred to Lisa. "Did you undress me the night I got sick?"

"No, you were in bed when I got here." Without noticing Lisa's pink cheeks, she unbuttoned the jacket and started to slip the gown over her head. When Lisa protested, the nurse said crisply, "You're being ridiculous, Miss Brooks. I know what's going through your mind but you're wrong—those are ribbons attached, not strings. Take it from me, Mr. Marshall doesn't have to buy girlfriends. His problem is keeping them out of the shrubbery."

"I know he's very handsome, but—"

"That doesn't have anything to do with it," Mrs. Dempster interrupted, "although I guess it's a plus. But even if he looked like Quasimodo, they would flock around."

"I don't understand."

"Do you mean to say you don't know who he is?"

Lisa shook her head but before the woman could enlighten her, the object of their discussion appeared in the doorway. He was wearing an impeccably tailored, dark, pin-striped suit, but he had removed his tie and unbuttoned the first few buttons of his white silk shirt, revealing a strong, bronzed column of neck.

Mrs. Dempster had just finished tying a length of satin ribbon around Lisa's hair and his eyes rested appreciatively on her hair's shining length before moving to her creamy shoulders. "I see the gown came. Is the color all right?"

"It's beautiful, but you really shouldn't have." Her fingers nervously touched the lace. "Now I owe you for this in addition to all the rest and I have no idea when I'll be able to repay you."

"Don't you think it's rather ungracious to offer to pay for a gift?" He pulled a straight chair up to the bed and the nurse tactfully left the room.

"Why should you give me a gift? You don't even know me."

Something kindled deep in his eyes as they swept over her slender figure, lingering for a moment on the curve of her breast, rising and falling more rapidly now under his enigmatic gaze. "Perhaps I know you better than you think."

"Who are you, Mr. Marshall?" she asked abruptly.

"Logan, please."

"All right . . . Logan. But please tell me who you are. I get the impression that I'm supposed to know you but I don't," she said helplessly.

"First, tell me who you are, Lisa."

"You know who I am."

"Only your name and why you came to California. You mentioned a job. What do you do?"

"I'm a secretary—or at least I was. My father was a professor of history at a private college in Texas. He also wrote books and I did research for him besides typing up his manuscripts."

"You said you *were* a secretary. Did you come to Hollywood because you wanted to get into a different line of work?" He waited intently for her answer.

"No, I told you why I left Abilene." Remembered pain darkened her eyes but she took a deep breath and lifted her chin. "Actually, it came as a shock when I wasn't able to get secretarial work here. I've taken a sales job in a department store to tide me over but I left my name at a number of agencies and I'm hoping something will turn up. I'm really a very good secretary," she said plaintively.

"I'm sure you are." He was still watching her closely. "Have you ever wanted to become an actress?"

"An actress? Of course not!" Her laughter was incredulous.

"You're very beautiful," he murmured.

Her lashes fell before the light in his eyes. "Thank you, but I'm sure there's a lot more to it than that. Acting is a profession, like teaching or carpentry. You have to study for it, you don't just decide to take it up."

"That's an interesting theory."

She dismissed the subject as unimportant. "Now it's your turn. What do you do?"

His blue eyes narrowed. "I'm the head of Magnum Studios."

"You make movies?" she asked. He nodded curtly without saying anything, but his watchful manner seemed to indicate that more was expected from her. "That must be . . . um . . . very interesting," she said politely.

Logan's eyes glinted with amusement. Unexpectedly, he took her hand and kissed the palm. "Lisa, you're too good to be true." The laughter died as he inspected her delicately boned face, lingering on the full generous mouth. "I wonder how long you will remain this way."

A small cough preceded a light rap at the door and Rogers, the butler, said, "Excuse me, sir, but there's a phone call for you."

Logan stood up, looking down at Lisa for a long minute. "Brian told me not to stay too long and I've probably exceeded the limit. I'll see you tomorrow, Lisa. Sleep well."

She stared after his receding back with a small sense of

loss. He seemed to charge the very air with electricity. What a strange man he was—sometimes almost forbidding, at other times utterly charming. But always vital and disturbing.

If the doctor took her pulse right now, he would be very displeased, Lisa thought with amusement. Not that she was actually attracted to Logan or anything silly like that. He was fantastically handsome of course, his dark good looks exuding a kind of animal magnetism that made him both dangerous and exciting. But he lived in a completely different world. Wouldn't she be an idiot to risk an emotional involvement with a man whose life read like one of his own scenarios?

It was finally clear what Mrs. Dempster had been trying to tell her. The name Logan Marshall hadn't rung a bell when he first gave it, but with the addition of Magnum Studios it certainly did!

Lisa recalled reading about Logan's exploits in gossip columns that hadn't been very kind to him. They pictured him as cruel and ruthless, crushing anyone who got in his way and discarding mistresses like Kleenex. There was even a scandal about a starlet who was supposed to have tried to commit suicide over him.

And yet look how kind he had been to Lisa, a perfect stranger. His anger when he thought she was trying to force her way in under false pretenses was understandable to her now, but could anyone have been gentler when it all proved a mistake?

There was no longer any doubt that he was the one who had undressed her, yet he hadn't tried to take advantage of the situation. A small pulse started to beat at the base of her throat as little things started coming back to her—how gentle his hands were and the soothing way he had stroked her bare shoulder. Her cheeks burned as she vaguely remembered that after he removed her clothes, she was the one who had snuggled up against him, unconsciously seeking warmth and comfort from that vital male body.

Even a less virile man might have gotten ideas! Thank heavens he knew she wasn't responsible for her actions.

Where was he going tonight—and with whom? Unconsciously, Lisa sighed, realizing that she couldn't expect him to spend his time with her. He said he would stop by the following day but if he actually did, it would probably be for a brief few minutes.

She glanced around, seeing evidence of Logan's kindness everywhere she looked—flowers, books and magazines, the very nightgown she wore. And last but certainly not least, this beautiful room with a nurse to cater to her every need.

Lisa made a decision. Tomorrow, she would be quite firm with that doctor. It would never do to get used to all this.

Chapter Two

In spite of Lisa's avowed intentions, it was Brian, abetted by Logan, who was firm with *her*.

"We will not even discuss the matter of your leaving here for at least a week, is that clear?" When she started to protest, he said blandly, "There is another alternative, of course. I could call an ambulance and have you taken to a hospital."

Logan turned on him sharply but Lisa didn't notice. She was too upset. "That would cost a fortune! I couldn't possibly afford it."

"Then I suppose you'll have to stay here," Brian said.

"But it isn't fair to Logan," she cried.

"I haven't complained," he said mildly.

"That's because you're so nice." When Brian snorted with laughter, Lisa confronted him indignantly. "Well, he is! How would *you* like to have a perfect stranger disrupting your house?"

"Is that an offer?" Brian teased. Turning to Logan, he asked innocently, "Would you like me to take her off your hands?"

"Will you stop upsetting her?" Logan scowled.

"Her, or you?" Brian asked slyly.

Ignoring him, Logan looked down at Lisa. "I can assure

you, you're no trouble. Not even to the servants. That's what Mrs. Dempster is for."

The woman was out of the room so Lisa felt free to speak. "That's another thing—I don't need a nurse. Won't you please let her go? When I think what all this is costing, I could jump out of my skin."

"I don't know why you have this ridiculous fixation about money," Logan said impatiently.

"Because I don't *have* any," she practically shouted at him. "And you two won't let me out of here so I can earn some."

"There is such a thing as being too independent. I'm surprised you haven't offered to pay me room and board," Logan said disgustedly.

Taking a deep breath, Lisa tried again. These two strong men were too much for her in her weakened condition, but she had to effect a compromise at least. "If I agree to stay for a week, will you let Mrs. Dempster go?"

Logan looked inquiringly at Brian, who shrugged. "I don't see why not. It's probably better than having her worry herself into a decline."

Lisa was elated but she soon found that she had won only a minor point. She was to stay in bed and take care of herself or the nurse would make a speedy return.

The days that she thought would drag passed speedily, to her surprise. Logan paid her a visit every morning, and the rest of the day she was still weak enough to appreciate just lying in bed reading and dozing.

At first, Lisa was worried about the added work for the servants since Brian and Logan were adamant that she have her meals in bed. But that worry was soon laid to rest. Mrs. Swensen, the placid, corpulent housekeeper, was happy to have a houseguest. She was a marvelous cook and since Logan was rarely home for dinner, she delighted in devising little treats to tempt Lisa's flagging appetite.

"You are nothing but skin and bones," she said disapprovingly. "See that she cleans her plate, Lucy," Mrs. Swensen told the sturdy young housemaid who brought up the trays.

Lucy was only too pleased to sit with the patient and her conversation was mostly about her employer, whom she obviously adored. "When I first got the job, I had mixed feelings," she confided. "You know—all that stuff you read about Mr. Marshall in the paper. Well, a girl is bound to wonder. But I must say he's always been a perfect gentleman," she said wistfully.

Lisa looked at her earnest, homely face and smothered a smile. A man like Logan probably didn't even notice that Lucy was female.

With her books, and Lucy and Mrs. Swensen's visits, the days passed pleasantly enough. But it was the nights that Lisa began to look forward to. Logan stopped in every evening after work and she made it a point to have her hair brushed until it gleamed like satin, not really wanting to examine the reasons why.

In the beginning he stayed only a short time, and when he left Lisa was achingly lonely, feeling that the evening was over, even though it might only be eight o'clock. But realizing that she had no claim on his time, she merely nodded when he said, "I suppose I'd better let you rest."

One night toward the middle of the week, the pattern changed. This time, Logan came into her room in tight-fitting jeans that molded to his muscular thighs, instead of one of the sober business suits he wore to the office or the elegant evening clothes that proclaimed he was off for a night on the town. A black turtleneck sweater hugged his broad shoulders and chest, underscoring the power of his lean torso.

"Are you going to a barbecue?" she asked doubtfully.

"What gives you that impression?" He smiled.

"The places you go always seem to be dress-up."

"I'm not going out tonight," he informed her. "Do you feel up to my company?"

"It . . . that would be very nice, but you mustn't feel you have to entertain me."

He looked at her for a long moment. "Did you ever think it might be the other way around?"

Her emerald eyes were confused. "I don't understand."

"I sometimes wonder if this isn't an act you're putting on for me, Lisa. Nobody could be that naive."

A little shiver ran down her spine and she pulled the covers up to her chin. All the things she had read about this man ran through her mind. Was there to be a final payoff after all? "Why would you want to be with me?" she asked, playing for time. "You know women a lot more fascinating."

"Have you ever met any of them?"

"No, of course not, but they must be. They've been all over the world. They can . . . well . . . talk about interesting things."

"And you can't?"

"Sure, if you want to know about the fact that the Pilgrims didn't really eat turkey on Thanksgiving." She grinned suddenly.

His dark eyebrows peaked. "I didn't know that. Why not?"

"Because the only turkeys then were wild ones and the Pilgrims had blunderbusses, not rifles. If they had ever happened to hit one, all they would have gotten were feathers."

A smile warmed his autocratic features. "You see, you've taught me something I wasn't aware of."

"I don't know what good it's going to do you. It's a little hard to work into the conversation." She laughed ruefully.

"You just managed it, didn't you?"

He was completely relaxed, with one leg thrown over the arm of an easy chair, his head resting on the back. He gave every appearance of being set for the evening but Lisa was sure he would soon become bored. Her mind whirled desperately in an effort to dredge up things that would amuse him. "Did you ever hear of Albert Packer, the only man ever accused of cannibalism in this country?"

With a ripple of muscles like the lithe movement of a panther, Logan got up from the chair and came to sit on the edge of the bed. "Why do I make you so nervous, Lisa?"

"It's . . . you . . . I never met anyone like you," she stammered.

"That makes us even."

"Then why aren't *you* nervous?"

"How do you know I'm not?" he asked wryly.

Lisa couldn't meet the flame in his eyes and she ducked her head. "Would you like to play gin rummy?" she asked unexpectedly.

Logan threw back his head and laughed until tears came to his eyes. "No one would ever believe it," he chuckled. "In fact, *I* don't believe it!" Hugging her to him briefly, he said, "I'd love to play gin rummy."

They played cards on the wide king-sized bed, bickering amiably as Logan's score rose. "It's only because you're getting all the cards," Lisa complained.

He looked at her petulant face with a secret smile. "You might as well get used to it, emerald eyes, I always win—sooner or later."

In the heat of competition, Lisa forgot her self-consciousness and was as relaxed as he. It was the most fun she had had in a long time, but when she tried to stifle a yawn about ten o'clock, Logan gathered the cards together.

"It's time you went to sleep," he said.

"I'm not tired, honestly," she protested.

Logan pulled the covers up to her chin and traced the line of her cheek with one long forefinger, his intent blue eyes fastened on the full mouth. For a heart-stopping moment, Lisa thought he was going to kiss her but he merely said, "I'll give you a rematch tomorrow."

The memory of that evening stayed with Lisa all the next day, even though she tried to reason with herself. The fact that he had spent it with her didn't mean anything. Even a sophisticated man about town took a night off every now and then. He had seemed to enjoy himself, but that was because it was such a novelty. Those parting words that he would give her a rematch were only a courtesy. He wouldn't care to repeat the experience and she mustn't attach such importance to it. As a matter of fact, it was a good thing she was leaving in a few days. Logan's visits were getting to be the high point of her day, which was the height of lunacy.

Lisa was so convinced Logan would take up his former pursuits that it was a shock when he appeared that night with a deck of cards in his hands.

"Are you ready for another lesson?" he asked teasingly.

Rallying her startled wits, she smiled brightly. "Only if I keep score this time."

It was while Logan was shuffling the cards that Lisa brought up a matter that was on her mind. "Logan, could I ask you for a tremendous favor?"

His hands stilled for a moment and then resumed riffling the cards. "Of course."

"You've done so much for me already that I hesitate to ask."

His face was expressionless. "Don't let that stop you."

"I don't suppose I should bother you with it since you'll be rid of me in a few days anyway."

"Will you get to the point, Lisa?" His mouth was a grim line.

He looked so forbidding that she was sorry she had started it, but it was too late now. "I'm awfully tired of lying around in nightgowns. I just wondered if you could stop by my apartment and get some clothes for me to wear. It's high time I got out of bed." His expression was so strange that she hurried on. "It isn't really important. As a matter of fact, I guess it was a dumb idea. My place is way across town and it would be terribly inconvenient for you."

Powerful emotions warred on Logan's face. "That's all you wanted to ask me for?"

"Please forget the whole thing," she begged. "It wasn't worth mentioning."

Taking both of her hands in his, he held them tightly. "You're very good for me, Lisa. You remind me that there is a whole other world besides the one I live in." When she looked at him uncomprehendingly, he said, "I'll go to your apartment first thing in the morning and pick up some clothes for you. Do you have an evening gown?"

Her puzzlement showed. "Yes, a long green chiffon. Why?"

"Because tomorrow night you're coming downstairs. We're going to have a champagne dinner by candlelight."

"Oh, Logan, that would be wonderful! I was beginning to feel as if I was born in this room and I was going to die here. Not that it isn't perfectly lovely," she added hurriedly.

"I know what you mean, honey," he chuckled. "But tomorrow night is your coming-out party."

A suitcase was delivered to Lisa the next morning and when she unpacked it, her eyes widened. If Logan had indeed selected these things, she didn't know what he was thinking. Her week would be up in two days and there were enough clothes here for three times that many. Oh well, men didn't know much about things like that. He probably grabbed everything he could lay his hands on.

After hanging up the green chiffon, she spent most of the afternoon getting ready. First, she washed her hair, and then soaked in a scented tub until her skin was rosy. Cobwebby stockings and lace underthings had been included. When her long eyelashes were curled and a lip gloss applied, there was no need for blusher. Lisa's eyes were sparkling as she smoothed the gown over her slim hips. It was slightly loose because of the weight she'd lost, but there were still enough curves to fill the draped bodice. When Logan tapped on the door a short time later, his appreciative eyes confirmed that fact.

"I think I'd better carry you down the stairs," he said.

"Certainly not! Ladies who are invited to champagne candlelight dinners should be able to navigate under their own power."

"At least at the beginning of the evening," he agreed gravely, although there was a wicked twinkle in his eyes.

They went into the den for a cocktail first and Lisa looked around with interest. "It's really a beautiful room isn't it?"

"You sound surprised," he said dryly. "But then, I suppose your first impression wasn't calculated to endear."

"You were both a little overwhelming," she admitted.

"Both? I thought I was the only ogre."

"Actually, it was Brian who drove me over the edge. When he told me to lie down on the couch . . ."

"All your mother's warnings came back full force," he supplied mockingly.

Lisa colored and changed the subject. "You've both been so good to me. Whatever Brian's bill is, it's worth it. And of course I'm going to pay you back for Mrs. Dempster." He started to interrupt but she wouldn't let him. "No, please don't argue with me. I probably don't have a job left after all this time, but I'll get another one. I'm going to repay both of you, even though it will have to be in installments."

"That's what I want to talk to you about, Lisa."

She shook her head. "I don't want to hear it. I didn't realize it at the time, but you very possibly saved my life."

He cupped her chin in his hand, looking deep into her eyes. "The Chinese have a theory. They believe if you save someone's life, you're responsible for them."

His touch was gentle, yet it evoked a response that was shocking. The blood thundered in her veins as Lisa's treacherous body yearned for more from his caressing fingers. It took a great effort to shake off the emotion that was enveloping her, but she murmured, "We're not Chinese."

"I want to take care of you, Lisa. Won't you let me?"

Her heart was racing and Lisa's long lashes brushed her cheeks. With any other man, the meaning of those words would have been clear, but Logan had demonstrated in many subtle ways that his interest in her was platonic. With all the opportunities that abounded, he hadn't even kissed her. The kindness he had shown was the sometimes authoritative, sometimes teasing kind that you give a kid sister. And that wasn't what Lisa wanted. For perhaps the first time, she began to realize that her interest in Logan was threatening to get out of hand.

With that in mind, she moved a safe distance away from him. "When my father died and I lived through that, I knew I could face anything. You don't have to worry about me, I'll get by."

"Doing what? Selling in a department store?"

"It pays the rent." She grinned suddenly. "Maybe I'll write a book. A comedy about all the size sixteen fat ladies who insist they can squeeze into a size eight."

"I have a better idea. Why don't you come to work for me?"

She raised her eyebrows. "Doing what? From what I can see, your every need is already fulfilled."

"That's a provocative statement if ever I heard one," he said mockingly.

"You know what I mean," she said uncomfortably. "Your house runs like a well-oiled machine and your office probably more so."

"Usually. But as a matter of fact, my private secretary just asked for a month's leave. Her daughter in New York is expecting any minute and it will be the first grandchild. Evidently a very big event."

"I should imagine so," Lisa agreed. "But I'm sure you have a whole office pool to draw from."

"Certainly. But you've been flinging around all this big talk about being such a super secretary. I thought I'd call your bluff."

"I *am* a good secretary!"

"Then why are you afraid to take the job for a month?"

"I'm not afraid. I only . . . I mean, I didn't want you to feel . . ."

"You'd really be doing me a favor, Lisa."

"Do you honestly mean it?" Her eyes shone. "You're not just being nice again?"

The corner of his mouth lifted derisively. "You heard Brian's opinion of that when you accused me of it in front of him."

"He was only kidding around, I realized that."

Logan took her hand, looking at her steadily. "I really need you, Lisa."

She gave him a dazzling smile. "In that case, I'd be delighted!"

"Then it's all settled. Finish your sherry before Mrs. Swensen's dinner is ruined. She's been cooking up a storm all day."

"She's a wonderful cook. It's a good thing I'm leaving soon, she's been fattening me up like a Christmas goose."

His eyes swept her slender body and something kindled deep in their depths, but he merely remarked, "I think you can stay for a few more pounds yet."

"That's another thing, Logan. My week's about up and I'd like to get my apartment in order. It must be a mess. When would you want me to start?"

He frowned. "There's no hurry."

"I thought you said your secretary was leaving."

"I can always make do with temporary help until you're completely well," he said smoothly.

"But I am! Let's see, this is Thursday—if I leave tomorrow, that will give me a long weekend to get straightened around. I can start on Monday." At his formidable expression, she wheedled, "That's *almost* a week."

"We'll see," he said noncommittally.

Rogers announced dinner at that point and they went

into the dining room, which Lisa had not seen previously. It was a dramatic room dominated by a long table fashioned from a length of rose-veined marble. Flocked wallpaper added elegance, along with a massive crystal chandelier which was dimmed now in deference to the twin silver candelabra alight with glowing candles.

The table was set as though for a state dinner, with flowered Coalport china, numerous sterling utensils, and several wineglasses at each place setting.

"My goodness, it looks like a banquet," Lisa exclaimed. "Shouldn't we have about a dozen other people?"

"Is that what you'd prefer? It's a little late but I imagine I could manage to scare up a party," Logan said dryly.

"No, I was only joking." She realized that part of the excitement of this evening was having Logan all to herself one last time.

Rogers poured white wine into her fluted Baccarat glass and Lisa smiled up at him. His manner was so different now that it didn't seem possible he was the same man who had frightened her so badly that fateful night she appeared, dripping, on the doorstep.

Lisa had no previous experience with butlers, but she was sure Rogers was the perfect one. He was never intrusive, yet each course appeared at exactly the right moment, and their wineglasses were filled the minute they were even slightly depleted.

They had reached the main course before Lisa gathered enough courage to ask Logan, "Why don't you ever talk about your work?"

"I don't want to bore you."

"How could you? Show business must be fascinating."

"Not my end of it." He shrugged. "It's mostly hard work."

"But that's what I want to hear about—what you do."

"If you really want to know, I deal in money and properties. Scripts," he amended at her puzzled look. "I have the final say on what gets produced and what doesn't. After making a decision, I try to pick the best people for the job. Then I convince the bankers to rely on my judgment."

"I see," she said uncertainly.

The steady blue eyes were mocking. "I'm sure you don't. Your idea of moviemaking is giant sound stages filled with beautifully costumed people waiting for the director to shout, 'Quiet everyone, this is a take.'"

"Isn't that the way it happens?"

"Sure—after interminable waits between scenes while they kill the lights and then set up again. Have you ever been on a movie set?" When she shook her head, Logan said, "It's about as much fun as watching paint dry."

Lisa took a sip of the excellent red wine that accompanied the beef. "I can scarcely believe that. Why would all those people try so desperately to break into movies?"

He shrugged. "Money . . . fame . . . a childish desire to show off."

"You don't like actors very much, do you?"

His mouth twisted wryly. "Let's say they're a necessary evil."

Lisa absently drained her glass. "I don't think you're being fair. It must be great fun—like playing dress-up and make-believe when you're a child."

Logan's eyes narrowed dangerously. "But they're not children, that's the point. They are grown men and women who are willing to sell their souls—and their bodies—for the fickle applause of a public who will turn its back on them tomorrow."

"Not always. How about the truly great actors, like the Barrymore family and Sarah Bernhardt? They dedicated their lives to the theater and were stars till the end."

"I wasn't referring to performers of that caliber. They had real talent and worked hard at perfecting their craft. Too many of the people in Hollywood today are trying to parlay a striking face and a willing body into stardom." His sensual lower lip thinned to a grim line. "Now do you understand my contempt?"

Lisa giggled suddenly. "All right, you've convinced me.

I won't become a movie star. May I have some more wine?"

His face relaxed as he took in her flushed cheeks and sparkling green eyes. "I think you're rapidly reaching the saturation point. Maybe black coffee would be a better idea."

She lowered her lashes, looking through them provocatively. "You promised me champagne."

Logan laughed and covered her hand with his. "All right, but go easy on the wine."

During the rest of the meal, Lisa finally managed to find out a little bit about Logan's personal life, details he jealously tried to guard from the tabloids. A reference to his sister elicited the information that she lived in England.

"Do you have any other family?" Lisa asked.

"Just my mother. She's visiting Madeleine in London right now but she should be home soon."

"Does she live here with you?"

"Scarcely." His mouth curved with amusement. "A man of thirty-eight needs his own establishment, wouldn't you say?"

Especially one as virile as you, Lisa thought, unable to meet the mocking light in his eyes.

Rogers brought in a silver ice bucket on a stand and Logan said, "Here's your champagne as promised. Would you like to have it in front of the fire in the den?"

"That would be lovely," she agreed as he pulled back her chair.

The dinner had been delicious and Lisa felt warm and relaxed. She seemed to float effortlessly over the thick carpet, her feet barely touching the floor. It was a delightful feeling, but when she took Logan's arm, smiling dreamily up at him, he cocked a concerned eyebrow at her. "Do you feel all right?"

"I feel *wonderful!*" She spread her arms and whirled around, which proved to be a mistake. When she stopped, the room didn't.

"I think we'll save the champagne for tomorrow night," he said, lifting her in his arms.

"Oh no, Logan, I'm fine." But her head was spinning and she had to cling to him until it stopped.

"You will be in the morning," he assured her, starting up the steps.

"Where are you taking me?"

"To bed," he said firmly.

"But it's still early! I don't want to ruin the party," she wailed into his shoulder. "And I didn't have my champagne."

In a voice choked with suppressed laughter, he said, "I'll bring it to you in the morning—if you can face it."

"You think I'm drunk," she protested tearfully.

"Of course not, darling." His lips brushed her forehead. "You're just not feeling up to par."

"I guess you're right." She sighed, clasping her arms around his neck and closing her eyes.

When Logan carried her into her room and set her gently on the bed, Lisa promptly curled into a little ball. She didn't bother with what he was saying because his voice seemed to come from a great distance.

Shaking her gently, Logan repeated it. "You'd better get undressed."

Her feathery brows drew together. "I don't feel like it."

Gentle hands raised her so that her back zipper could be undone, then Logan lifted her into his lap while he removed the long gown. "This is getting to be a habit," he chuckled.

Suddenly the mists cleared and Lisa was conscious of the sensuous feel of strong male hands on her bare skin. She could feel the warmth of his body and smell the clean masculine aroma of English soap mixed with tobacco and something else. The relaxed, languorous feeling disappeared, replaced by something primitive and compelling. A flame started below her waist and swept upward, threatening to devour her. It was unlike anything she had ever experienced and when Logan put an arm under her knees, preparatory to sliding her into bed, she clung tightly to him.

His own arms tightened for a moment, then loosened as he said in a husky voice, "Let go, darling, so I can put you in bed."

She tilted her head back to look at him with eyes that were almost jade green with emotion. Without releasing her grip, Lisa whispered, "Don't leave me."

A flame leaped in his eyes as he studied the exquisite face with its slightly parted, trembling mouth. "You don't know what you're saying. You've had too much to drink," he said harshly.

"No, I haven't. Please stay with me, Logan."

His hands moved almost unwillingly, trailing down the long, lovely throat and over the softly swelling curves above the wispy bra. A swift thrill of desire shot through Lisa as she raised her face expectantly. But Logan was reaching up to try to disengage her arms. "Don't be a fool!" he bit out savagely. "You're drunk. I'm not the kind of man who would take advantage of it."

Tears filled her lovely eyes as she let him break her hold. "I'm not beautiful enough for you. You don't want me."

Logan gathered her in an embrace that threatened to crush her fragile bones. "Oh, God, if you only knew!"

She drew back just far enough to look at him and the molten passion on his face convinced her. Giving him a tremulous smile, she murmured, "Aren't you *ever* going to kiss me?"

With a groan of surrender, Logan covered her mouth. His lips demanded a response that Lisa was only too happy to give, and when he probed her mouth with a driving masculinity that she had never experienced before, she trembled with anticipation.

His hands wandered lovingly over her bare skin, setting her on fire. Soon his lips followed the path of his fingers, trailing a line of arousing kisses. Lisa trembled as Logan lifted his head to look at her body with glowing eyes, but she felt no embarrassment, only a mounting excitement. His warm mouth tasted each creamy breast lingeringly, evoking a cry of delight.

She helped him remove his shirt and when the long triangle of his splendid torso was exposed, Lisa pressed her lips to it. With a low, throaty sound, Logan put her down on the bed and covered her body with his. The feeling was inexpressible and she moved against him.

"I never knew it would be like this," she murmured, tasting the hollow of his neck.

"My beautiful angel," Logan whispered, tangling his fingers in her long red hair. Lisa lifted her mouth for his kiss, but suddenly the tide of passion was stemmed as he looked at her sharply. "What did you say?"

Lisa smiled at him dreamily. "I don't know. Kiss me, Logan."

"You said you didn't know it would be like this."

"Oh, yes. Is it always this wonderful, Logan?"

He sat up suddenly, his face austere. "Haven't you ever been with a man, Lisa?"

The change in him frightened her. "No, I . . . I've never . . . does it matter?" she pleaded.

"Does it *matter?*" He stood up and towered over her like an avenging angel. "I ought to beat the living daylights out of you! Do you know what you almost made me do?" He ran a savage hand through his thick hair. "My God, have I sunk so low that I'd take advantage of a tipsy virgin?"

Lisa sat up and pulled the covers over her naked body. "But you didn't. I was the one—"

"Go to sleep, Lisa."

With a desolation that was crushing, she watched his tall figure stride out the door. Had she really offered herself for the first time—and been turned down? Her mind cringed away from such a cruel rejection, even while her trembling body cried out for him.

But what had she expected? Logan had told her his opinion of "easy women," and she was one of the easiest!

The only tiny ray of salvation was that he thought she was drunk when she begged him to make love to her. But Lisa knew that wasn't the case. Maybe she had been a little high when he carried her upstairs, but when he held her in his arms, she had sobered instantly.

This was what she had been yearning for all week, even though it hadn't penetrated her consciousness. Or was it because she wouldn't allow it to? For days, Lisa had been fighting against the secret knowledge that she was falling in love with a man she could never have. Logan Marshall was as unobtainable as the North Star. He was rich and famous, handsome and sought after—and he had a low opinion of women. What would he think of her after tonight?

Lisa shuddered and covered her mouth with trembling fingers. The idea of those cruel blue eyes raking her with contempt was more than she could bear to think about. Would it make him more understanding if he knew she had fallen in love with him? No! That was something he musn't ever find out!

The only solution was never to see him again. After he left for work tomorrow, she would gather together every trace of herself and slip out of his house.

But even as the thought gave some measure of solace, Lisa knew that his memory would not slip out of her mind that easily.

Chapter Three

It was almost daylight before Lisa fell asleep, but even so, she was instantly awake when Logan came into her room the next morning. She was lying on her stomach, long hair tumbled over the silken coverlet, and she kept her eyes tightly closed when he approached the bed.

"Lisa?" he murmured softly, making it an effort for her to maintain the even breathing that would indicate she was asleep.

It was added torture when Logan's fingers smoothed the hair off her face and trailed gently down her cheek. Lisa was achingly conscious of him, his touch and feel, the crisp masculine scent of his aftershave, but she managed to remain motionless. After a long moment he left the room, and not until the door closed did she release her breath.

When a suitable time had elapsed, she jumped out of bed and started to dress. There was one tense moment when Lucy came in just as Lisa was about to pull her suitcase from the closet, but she shoved it back quickly.

"You're already dressed," the young maid said with surprise. "Mr. Marshall said not to disturb you till you rang. I was just peeking in to see if you were up yet."

"Oh . . . yes, I'm up."

"He said you might sleep late."

"Did . . . did he say anything else?" The words were forced out against Lisa's will.

"No, just to take good care of you and see that you had everything you wanted." Lucy looked at her enviously. "Mr. Marshall really likes you."

Lisa's breath caught in her throat. If she only knew! Turning away, she said, "You don't have to bother about breakfast this morning. I don't want any."

"Mr. Marshall won't like that," Lucy said disapprovingly.

"Let me worry about it," Lisa said sharply, and then was sorry when the girl gave her a hurt look.

It didn't take long to stuff all her things in the suitcase, and after a quick look around to be sure she hadn't forgotten anything, Lisa opened the door quietly. This was the tricky part. She felt bad at not saying good-bye to the servants who had been so kind to her, but there were bound to be questions about her unexpected departure that she didn't feel up to answering.

Several days earlier, Logan had told her the Morris had been patched together once more and was stored in his garage. When he handed her the keys, he had remarked disapprovingly that it was a pile of junk and she ought to get rid of it. She had been forced to agree with him, but now she regarded it in an entirely different light. The battered little car was her means of escape. That was another expense though. She owed Logan for its repairs.

The small apartment, miles from the rarefied atmosphere of Logan's house, looked shabby after her luxurious living quarters. Glancing at the worn sofa, Lisa couldn't help comparing it with the soft, down-filled one in Logan's den. But inevitably, that brought back thoughts of him which she had come home to avoid. The thing to do was to occupy her mind so thoroughly that there would be no room in it for Logan.

Everything was dusty and had an unlived-in look, and

Lisa set to work cleaning, scrubbing and polishing. She worked so obsessively that by late afternoon the little place sparkled. After taking a shower and washing her hair, she realized for the first time how tired she was. Today had been quite different from being waited on hand and foot, but the sooner she forgot about that the better, Lisa decided grimly.

Choosing a long, flowered housecoat instead of bothering to get dressed again, she brushed her long hair until it glowed like an autumn leaf. With a face carelessly free of makeup, she looked about fourteen years old.

Padding barefoot into the living room, Lisa considered making herself something to eat and then rejected the idea. Although she hadn't eaten all day, the couch looked so inviting that she decided to rest for a while first. Her eyes closed and the next thing she was conscious of was the doorbell pealing insistently.

The room was in darkness and for a moment Lisa was disoriented. She stumbled to the door, but the mists of sleep were abruptly dissipated as she focused on Logan. "What are you doing here?" she mumbled.

He looked at her evenly. "I might ask you the same thing."

"What are you talking about? I *live* here."

A look of impatience crossed his autocratic face. "Do we have to stand in the doorway like this?"

Lisa stepped aside reluctantly so Logan could enter the living room, his presence seeming to make it even smaller. Seeing him so unexpectedly made the blood race through her veins and she put a hand up self-consciously to smooth her riotous hair. His eyes followed the motion, lingering on the shining auburn waves before moving to rest on her tremulous mouth.

"Why did you run away, Lisa?" he asked finally.

"I didn't run away," she said, carefully inspecting the knot in his tie. "The week that we agreed on was almost up. I just left a little early, that's all."

"Without a word to anyone? Mrs. Swensen and Lucy were very worried. They didn't know what happened to you."

"Oh . . . well . . . I'm sorry about that."

"And how about me?" he asked severely. "I left this morning expecting to find you there when I returned. Don't you think it would have been courteous to at least say good-bye?"

"I thought it would be easier this way," she said miserably. "I didn't think you'd want me around anymore."

"That's interesting. What gave you that impression?"

"Oh, Logan, stop torturing me! We both know what we're talking about."

He didn't pretend to misunderstand. "You mean last night."

"Yes." She couldn't look at him. "I know what you think of me."

"Are you sure?" he asked quietly.

Lisa bit her lip. "You've made it abundantly clear how you feel about women who use their bodies to get something from a man."

His grim mouth relaxed in a wry smile. "I wasn't talking about motives like yours." Her cheeks flamed and she ducked her head but he raised it with a long forefinger, forcing her to look at him. "You would never have to make a trade, Lisa. If you wanted anything from me, all you'd have to do is ask."

"I never wanted anything from you," she said indignantly.

"I know, not even my—"

"Please, Logan, I'd rather not talk about it," she interrupted, feeling like a fraud. There *was* something she wanted, something he couldn't give—his love.

"You mustn't be so upset, honey." His hands were gentle on her shoulders. "It isn't a crime to have a little too much wine. Actually, it was my fault. I should have realized your weakened condition."

His nearness was making breathing difficult. Why did he have to be so tall and masculine and completely in command of himself? "I did more than that," she murmured.

"You have nothing to reproach yourself for, Lisa," he said quietly. "Nothing happened."

"No thanks to me, was it?" Her voice was muffled.

He gave her a little shake. "Why do you insist on punishing yourself? You aren't the first person to experience natural urges. The fact that you haven't given in to them sooner is to your credit." Lisa could have told him she didn't deserve his praise. Logan was the first man she had ever wanted and she had a terrible feeling she would never get over that desire. He lifted her chin once more, his eyes searching as they scanned her troubled face intently. "It's just fortunate that I found out in time. You have a wonderful gift to bestow, my dear, it should be given to someone you love."

Her eyes were a shimmer of green behind lowered lashes. Lisa didn't dare look at him for fear he would see what had to remain secret. "What if I never fall in love?"

"You will," he said confidently.

She shook her head. "I doubt it. No man ever interested me that much," she lied.

"I can't believe there haven't been boyfriends."

She shrugged, remembering the urgent young men in Abilene. None of them had managed to touch her emotions and now she realized why. They were just boys compared to this dynamic man. There was no one like Logan; that was the tragedy. Having known him, she could never settle for second best.

"There must have been a lot of men in your life," he insisted.

"I go out on dates," she acknowledged, "but there's nobody special. Maybe because I don't want there to be."

"Don't you want to get married, Lisa?" There was a stillness about him as he waited for her answer.

She swallowed hard. "No way. If a man got serious

about me, I'd run in the opposite direction." That at least was the truth. Anyone but Logan.

His eyes were wintry. "I see. Well, it's nice to meet a woman who knows her own mind."

"You wanted me to be truthful, didn't you?" she asked, holding her breath. Everything depended on Logan's believing her.

"Of course." A long forefinger traced the shape of her mouth for a moment before he said briskly, "All right, get your things together now and we'll go home."

Her startled eyes flew to his face and she began to laugh unwillingly. "I *am* home, remember?"

His disdainful glance flicked over the small apartment. "You aren't ready to take care of yourself yet." He looked at her sharply. "There are shadows under your eyes and you look tired. You're coming back to my place and having dinner in bed tonight."

"You're out of your mind! I've been in bed too much, that's the whole trouble." Coloring slightly, she continued, "I have to get back to normal so I can go back to work."

"There's no hurry about that. I don't want you coming in until you really feel up to it," he warned.

It hadn't occurred to Lisa that he would still expect her to work for him. "I can't take that job, Logan. Surely you can understand that," she pleaded.

"I don't understand anything of the sort. It was all agreed upon."

"I know, but if you don't mind, I . . . I think it would be better if I didn't."

"Better for whom?" he demanded. "I won't be churlish enough to remind you that you owe me something, but I find it difficult to understand how you can leave me in the lurch when I need you."

"If I thought you really did . . ."

"I do," he said curtly, an enigmatic expression in his eyes.

If it was really true, Lisa didn't know how to refuse.

"Well, in that case . . . what time would you like me Monday morning?"

After Logan was convinced that she felt fit enough, and after he accepted the fact that she wasn't returning to his house, he took a reluctant leave. When the door finally closed after him, Lisa felt like she had been put through a wringer. But there was a strange exhilaration too. For another whole month, she would continue to see him every day. It was like being given an unexpected gift.

She didn't even have to reproach herself for trying to cling to an impossible dream. Logan was the one who had been quite angry at her defection, so he must really need her. Why else would he insist she take the job?

On Monday morning, Lisa guided the trusty Morris into a parking space in front of a tall glass and steel building. Logan had left word with the uniformed guard, who opened the gates after a disparaging look at the little car. He also gave her grudging directions.

Lisa had never been inside a movie studio before, and she looked around with great interest. The tower where Logan had his office was the only tall building on the lot. On either side of it were a series of bungalows, like small homes, with parking spaces marked off in front of each one. The names of the occupants were printed on the curb but they were unfamiliar to Lisa. She found out later that these were offices, mostly occupied by production people. The huge, windowless, hangarlike buildings dotted about were easier to identify. As she correctly assumed, these were sound stages.

There was a tastefully landscaped square in front of a long, low commissary, and many of the people going in and out were dressed in costume. It was a jumble of periods. A Renaissance lady strolling with a man garbed as an American Indian stopped to chat with two men gotten up as nineteenth-century English sailors.

Lisa would have liked to have lingered to watch the show but, mindful of the time, she entered the modern

building and started for Logan's office. It was to be an
impeded progress. She already knew he was important,
but was even the President guarded like this? After
giving her name innumerable times, she passed through
each checkpoint and was finally whisked to the top
floor.

A very beautiful young woman was installed at a desk in
front of the door to the inner office. With an emotionless
face, she watched Lisa approach across a seemingly endless expanse of pale gray carpeting. Only when Lisa had
given her name did a flicker of emotion cross those perfect
features. There was an appraising quality to the heavily
made-up eyes as she pressed a key and murmured into an
intercom.

Almost immediately, an older woman appeared.
"Hello, I'm Mrs. Livingstone." She smiled. "Won't you
come in?"

Lisa followed her into a comfortable office with a
window that looked out over the studio and the hills
beyond. The large desk was piled with papers, but the rest
of the room was neat and held small touches that made it
seem homey.

After pleasantries had been exchanged, Logan's secretary told Lisa, "Mr. Marshall said I was to spend the day
showing you the ropes. I offered to stay longer but he said
you were a bright girl and would catch on quickly."

Lisa swallowed nervously. "I hope his confidence isn't
misplaced."

"I'm sure it isn't," the older woman said reassuringly.
"Would you like some coffee before we begin?"

"No, thank you. I think I'd like to get started, if you
don't mind."

"Right you are. Well, to begin with, these are the
primary things to remember."

For the next hour, she gave concise instructions, watching approvingly as Lisa took notes. It didn't seem like an
insurmountable job, especially since there were several

secretaries to take care of routine correspondence and type statistical reports.

"Another important part of your job will be to screen undesirables," Mrs. Livingstone continued. "Out-of-work actors and actresses are obvious of course, but you have to be careful of producers and directors too." A cynical smile curled her mouth. "You'll soon learn who is in and who is out. You will also take care of all confidential correspondence and phone calls, plus making any reservations required. I have a list of all Mr. Marshall's favorite restaurants and the names of the maître d's. Now where did I put that? Oh yes, here it is. It has the florist's number too."

Lisa was bewildered. "The florist?"

"You will be acting as Mr. Marshall's *personal* secretary," Mrs. Livingstone said gently.

"I see," Lisa said stiffly.

"Yes, well, I think that about covers it. Do you have any questions?"

There were about a dozen, but they weren't the kind she could ask. "No, you've explained everything very well. I think I'll be able to hold down the fort. You must be anxious to get on with your vacation."

"I really am. It was so nice of Mr. Marshall to give me the time off. A first grandchild is quite an event. Of course at your age, you're probably looking forward to your first child."

"Not exactly." Lisa grinned. "I'm not married."

The other woman looked at the auburn hair curling on her slim shoulders and the wide, thickly fringed green eyes. "You will be, my dear," she murmured.

Since Mrs. Livingstone had left instructions that they were not to be disturbed, they covered a lot of territory without wasting time. By early afternoon, there seemed no reason for Mrs. Livingstone to stay around and she left, amid good wishes on both sides.

But when the door closed after her, Lisa experienced a

moment of panic. And when the buzzer on her desk sounded, she jumped.

"Would you come in here, Lisa?" There was no mistaking that deep voice.

Logan's office was next door to hers and its splendor overwhelmed her. Except for a handsome desk positioned where two walls of windows met, it looked more like the living room in a mansion. A priceless tapestry hung over a long couch flanked by two upholstered chairs and a coffee table. At an angle from these was a round conference table surrounded by leather chairs. The remaining wall was lined with shelves containing art objects and richly bound books.

"This is gorgeous," Lisa gasped. "If I worked here, I don't think I'd ever go home!"

"You're welcome to stay over any time." Logan looked impossibly handsome in a charcoal suit that enhanced his immaculate shirt and elegant tie. He also looked very forbidding, but the impression was dispelled when he smiled. "There's a shower in there." He nodded toward a door that evidently led to a bathroom.

"It was only an observation," she said primly.

"I'm sure." His smile turned sardonic. "Did Mrs. Livingstone tell you everything you need to know?"

"Yes, I think so. She's very efficient. We seemed to cover everything in record time so she left early. I hope that was all right?" she asked anxiously.

He nodded indifferently. The phone at his elbow rang, but when Lisa started toward it, he stopped her. "That's my private line. No one else answers it." As she hovered uncertainly, Logan said, "I'll call you if I need you."

Feeling snubbed, Lisa went back to her own office. Was that the number his girlfriends used? she wondered.

A young man waiting in her office greeted her with an admiring whistle. "Well, well, where did you come from?"

"I'm Mr. Marshall's secretary."

"What happened to the dragon?" At her raised eyebrows, he said, "Mrs. Livingstone. She's a nice old gal but she guards the gates as though they were pearly."

"What makes you think I won't?"

"I wouldn't mind if you did. Hanging around here could get to be habit-forming."

"Who are you, Mr.—?"

"Chuck. Chuck Talbot, boy genius." When that produced a blank stare, he said, "Don't you read the trades? I've been tapped to direct Logan's new extravaganza, *Tropic Fever*."

"I'm sorry if I should know your name, but I'm new to the movie industry," Lisa apologized. "As a matter of fact, this is my first day."

"Think nothing of it, a lot of people don't know my name." He grinned. "But I hope you'll remember it. Since you're new at the job, I'd be happy to show you the ropes around here. How about having dinner with me tonight?"

The buzzer on Lisa's desk sounded before she could answer, and Logan's disembodied voice said, "When Chuck Talbot gets here, send him in."

"He's already here, Mr. Marshall."

Chuck leaned over her shoulder, speaking into the box. "Don't hurry on my account, Logan." He laughed. "I could kill quite a lot of time where I am."

There was a click, and Logan appeared so suddenly that Chuck was still bent over Lisa. Logan's eyes were chilly as they rested on the pair. "Your time might be worthless, but mine costs a great deal. If you're still interested in the project, perhaps you'll honor me with your presence."

Chuck whistled soundlessly, giving Lisa a speculative look as he followed Logan's rigid back.

It was almost quitting time when Logan stopped by her desk, his impatience with the director evidently forgotten. "How did everything go today?" He smiled. "Did you have any trouble?"

"No, it was a breeze. I'm really going to enjoy working here."

He eyed her eager face impassively. "That's good."

Then, almost curtly, "Mrs. Swensen told me to bring you home to dinner. She said you probably haven't had a decent meal since you left."

Lisa smiled. "That's nice of her, but will you offer my regrets and ask for a rain check?"

"You have another engagement?" He frowned. Before she could answer, the frown changed to a sarcastic smile. "That Chuck is a fast worker."

"What makes you think I'm going out with Chuck?" she asked indignantly.

"He didn't ask you for a date?"

"Well . . . as a matter of fact, he did."

"And you accepted without knowing anything about him?"

He was towering over her menacingly and Lisa stood up to face him, although she had to tilt her head back to do it. "For your information, I *didn't* accept." She didn't have the chance, as Chuck hadn't appeared back in her office, but Logan didn't have to know that.

His grim expression relaxed. "I know you think it's none of my business, Lisa, but I worry about you. You'd be like a babe in the woods with these ravening wolves."

She wanted to stamp her foot, but that would make her seem like the child he took her for. Why couldn't he see her as a woman? Still, he was acting out of a mistaken sense of duty.

Trying to curb her temper in recognition of all he had done for her, Lisa said, "Will you stop feeling responsible for me if I promise to be careful?"

"I believe that comes under the heading of famous last words."

She countered his skeptical look with a mischievous grin. "Tell you what, I won't accept a date with anyone until he brings me a character reference from his mother."

He smiled finally. "That ought to do it. And you'll reconsider about coming to dinner tonight?"

"No, to tell you the truth, I'm a little tired. It's my first day back at work and I thought I'd turn in early."

He was immediately concerned. "I told you it was too soon. You're to stay home tomorrow," he said decisively.

"Oh, Logan, don't be silly."

"Get your things together, I'm taking you home right now," he commanded.

"I have my car," she reminded him.

He frowned. "That's another thing. We'll have to do something about getting you decent transportation."

"*Logan!*" she cried warningly.

He scowled down at her exasperated face for a long moment before turning on his heel. "God save me from independent women!" he ground out, as he disappeared through the door.

Lisa found the work fascinating and the days flew by. It caused a pang every time she remembered that the job was only temporary, but she refused to dwell on that. As she learned more about Logan's position in the industry, her respect for him grew. The confidential correspondence she handled disclosed the amount of money involved and it widened her eyes. But her special delight was sitting in on conferences. That's where movies were planned and important details ironed out.

She also enjoyed eating lunch in the commissary and seeing famous people, who often greeted her warmly even though she might have met them only briefly. As Logan Marshall's secretary, she found that everyone went out of his way to be nice to her, and a lot of men asked her for dates. But mindful of the fact that they might be using her to get to Logan, she was cautious about accepting. And strangely enough, they never seemed to ask twice.

Lisa didn't really care though. The only man she wanted to be with was in the next office, and seeing him every day carried her through the nights. But there were hurtful times too. Often, Logan would casually ask her to send flowers to some woman or other. His expression was unreadable as he made the request and she tried to make hers as offhand, concealing the jealousy that sliced through her like a knife.

One day, he stopped by her desk. "There's going to be a conference this afternoon on the new picture and I'd like you to take notes."

It turned out to be a large conference with the director, the producer, the art director and numerous assistants. The starting date for the movie had been set and Logan was calling for reports.

"I think we have the location pretty well narrowed down to two choices," John Babcock, the producer, said. "Either Nuku'alofa in the Tongas or Pago Pago in Samoa."

The art director, whom Lisa knew only as Vince, was concerned. "Are they really tropical? Some of those islands, like Noumea, look like Pennsylvania with palm trees."

"Wait till you see these two places," John assured him. "You'll want to take off your clothes and go native."

"How about I take off my clothes and go *with* a native?" Chuck grinned.

"Gentlemen!" Logan cracked out.

"Sorry, Lisa," Chuck apologized.

"The question is, which location is better? What does one have to recommend it over the other?" Logan asked.

"I have the report right here," John said. "Our advance scout says they don't call Tonga the friendly islands for nothing. The natives are cooperative and they're beautiful people too—especially the children. We'll have to be sure and work in some shots of the kids," he digressed.

"And Pago Pago?" Logan asked.

"Well, it's bigger of course, and it has that fantastic harbor. But off the top of my head, I'd plunk for the Tongas."

"Nuku'alofa is too hard to pronounce," Chuck objected. "And everyone's heard of Pago Pago."

"I think the terrain is more important than the name," Vince said. "Does anyone have any pictures?"

"Just the usual publicity shots," John admitted, "and

those are chancy. You know what you can do with trick photography."

"I'm willing to settle for either one," Chuck said cheerfully. "After all, they're both in the South Seas—how bad can it be?"

Logan's look was frosty. "The budget on this picture precludes a game of eeny-meeny. As I see it, we have only one choice. We'll fly out there and take a look."

"Who is we, chief?" Chuck asked.

"All of us," Logan said crisply. "Everyone with a measure of responsibility for the production." He smiled mirthlessly. "In case of foul-ups, there won't be any buck to pass."

After the meeting broke up, Lisa's work began in earnest. Logan gave her a list of names and told her to call the traffic department to arrange for airline tickets.

"I think we'll fly into Pago Pago; I know they have a landing field. We'll charter a yacht from there. Have them arrange it and also book hotel rooms."

There were a lot more instructions and Lisa scribbled rapidly, thankful for her excellent shorthand. At last, Logan stopped biting out commands, but as she started toward the door, he stopped her.

"Do you have a passport?" he asked.

"A passport?" she repeated inanely.

"Yes, do you have one and is it up to date?"

"No. I mean no, I don't have one. I've never been anywhere to need it."

"That's what I was afraid of. All right, call the legal department and have them contact Washington and rush it through."

"But I don't understand. Why?"

"You *do* expect to come back to this country don't you? Or were you planning on going native with Chuck?"

Her mouth dropped open. "Do you mean that I . . . you . . . but I don't have anything to do with the picture!"

"But I do, and I need a secretary. Shorthand isn't one of my talents."

It's the only thing that isn't, Lisa thought, giving him a dazzling smile. "Oh, Logan, I'm so excited! I can hardly believe it!" Impulsively, she threw her arms around his neck, hugging him close. "Thank you, you're wonderful!"

His hands tightened around her waist for a moment before he set her away. "I told you, you didn't have to make a trade with me," he said harshly.

The eagerness in her eyes was replaced by hurt. When would she learn that any display of emotion on her part made him wary? It had only been an expression of exuberance, but it had triggered another rejection.

"I wasn't offering anything," she said stiffly. "If this trip is another one of your generosities, then count me out."

He jammed his hands in his pockets and said savagely, "Don't be a little idiot."

"You don't really need me, do you?" she asked dully.

"Of course I need you! Why else would I take you?"

Why else indeed? Lisa looked down at the notebook clutched so tightly in her hands and felt like crying. "In that case, I'll make the arrangements." She started for the door, stopping with her back to him. "And you needn't worry. In the future, I'll try to control my high spirits."

The look on his face would have puzzled her greatly.

Chapter Four

It was broad daylight when the plane swooped in for a landing at Pago Pago. As they made their approach, Lisa's spirits rose in direct opposition to the swift descent of the jet. She was actually in the South Seas!

Warm, balmy air greeted them, and through the windows of the customs shack she caught tantalizing glimpses of palm trees and tropic vegetation. The formalities seemed endless, yet it was actually just a short time before the company was herded into a small, rather ramshackle bus drawn up at the entrance to meet them.

The mundane conveyance surprised Lisa. Logan was always surrounded by such luxury that she expected a fleet of limousines, at the very least. The mocking look on his face as he helped her aboard, taking the seat next to hers, indicated that he had read her mind and was amused by it. He made no comment, however.

The narrow road that led to the hotel wound through lush countryside that fulfilled all of Lisa's expectations. Dense banks of tangled green bordered the bumpy highway, punctuated by bursts of riotous color where tropical flowers flaunted their insistent blooms.

Some were familiar, like the velvety hibiscus and the brilliant bougainvillea, but the frangipani trees were definitely exotic. Unlike any shrub Lisa had ever seen, they had gnarled limbs that were bare except for the very tips, which were feathered with oval leaves and delicate cream or pink petals. Against a background of clear green banana fronds, the effect was breathtaking.

Soon the junglelike growth gave way to small clearings with strange buildings—round, oval or rectangular in shape, yet all constructed in the same basic way. A thatched roof was supported every five or six feet by hand-hewn pillars, and the wooden platform that formed the floor was raised up off the ground.

"What on earth are those?" she cried.

"Those are called *fales*," the bus driver told her. "They are native houses."

Then she noticed that they were indeed furnished, although for the most part sparsely. A mattress with bed covers was placed right on the wooden floors and some had a small table and several straight chairs.

"But they don't have any windows or doors," she exclaimed.

"Don't need doors." Manuka, the driver, grinned. "Just walk right in."

"What happens when it rains?"

"Long woven blinds are rolled up under the roof," he explained. "Can be let down to close up *fale*. But most people, they like to sit and watch the world go by."

It was completely alien to the Western culture where privacy was almost a cult, yet what Manuka said seemed to be true. The natives lounging against the wooden supports watched the bus with interest, waving in a friendly fashion as they went past.

Lisa turned in her seat to wave back. "It's all so fascinating," she breathed.

"After you get settled at hotel, I take you to see the island," the driver offered, pleased by her enthusiasm.

"Thank you, I wish I could," Lisa said wistfully. "But I'm not on vacation."

"You aren't expected to work nonstop either," Logan said. "Of course you can go."

She shook her head. "It wouldn't be fair. Everyone else will be working. I don't expect special privileges."

"Suppose I went with you? Would that ease your conscience?"

"Oh, Logan, would you really?" Her happiness dimmed suddenly at the realization that his time was worth a lot of money, as he had once reminded Chuck. "I couldn't ask you to do that."

"You aren't asking me, it's the other way around." His eyes were the blue of the ocean as he smiled down at her. "As soon as we get some of this business out of the way, you and I will play hooky."

The prospect was so enchanting that Lisa found it difficult to concentrate on the scenery after that.

There was much confusion when they finally arrived at the hotel, a charming two-story building with a broad veranda. They were all assigned rooms, with instructions to be downstairs promptly in half an hour. The first order of the day was a visit to inspect the fabled Pago Pago harbor.

A whole fleet of cars had been put at their disposal, but after Lisa discovered that the harbor area was only a few short blocks from the hotel she exclaimed, "We could have walked!"

Logan raised a sardonic eyebrow. "I'm afraid you will never be a star, Lisa my love. Don't you know that movie people never do anything as mundane as walking?"

She gave him an impish grin. "If I promise to forgo a movie career, will you walk back with me?"

Putting his arm around her shoulders, he said, "It's a deal."

The dock area was impressive. Lisa had been told that the deepwater harbor was actually the crater of a volcano, and her imagination soared as she pictured the early Samoans discovering it for the first time. Those brooding, dark green cliffs must have been very formidable. Imagine the joy of those intrepid men in their small balsa-wood boats when they discovered an unexpected harbor with a gentle, smiling land beckoning to them.

"This is fantastic," Chuck was saying enthusiastically. "A tropic dream!"

"But how about those modern houses up the cliff?" Vince objected. "The story takes place in the early nineteen-hundreds."

Marsha Block, the production supervisor, was a dark-haired young woman with a thin, intelligent face. She turned now to Ted Huruska, the head cameraman. "No problem, is there, Ted? You can keep the camera angle low at that point, can't you?"

When he agreed, Chuck said, "This is it then. What do you think, chief?"

"I think there are a lot of other things we have to find out," Logan said crisply.

While the crew investigated the dock area, Lisa wandered around admiring the magnificent view. The sun was shining brightly in a tropical sky of burning blue decorated with white fleecy clouds. It cast diamond sparkles on the calm water of the harbor. When her dazzled eyes focused, Lisa saw tiny rainbow-colored fish swimming near the surface. Swinging her legs over the wooden wharf, she perched on the edge, peering in fascination.

"What are you looking at?" Logan's deep voice inquired.

"You should see all the fish down there! And look, Logan—what is that kind of transparent-looking round one with sort of ribbons trailing after it?"

He hunched down next to her. "That's a squid."

"I thought they were great big things."

"There are giant ones, but I believe you are thinking of octopus. The small squid are considered quite a delicacy in these parts. I'm sure you will get a chance to sample them."

Lisa gazed doubtfully at the rather unappetizing-looking creature. "Maybe I'll just skip it."

"I thought you were the liberated woman who was game for anything," he teased.

"I've just discovered that my stomach isn't as liberated as the rest of me." She laughed.

Logan helped her to her feet. "Are you ready for that walk now? I'll take you to see something of the town."

It was actually more like a sleepy little village. Small shops displaying brightly patterned clothing were wedged in next to general stores whose fly-specked windows contained everything from aspirin to woven baskets. Handsome people ambled along in colorful native dress, crossing the street whenever the fancy took them since there were no traffic lights. Their white teeth gleamed in laughing brown faces as they dodged in and out among the infrequent cars. In the center of town, a tremendous *fale* served as an open-air market.

"The fishermen bring their catch here very early in the morning," Logan explained. "At this hour of the day all they have are fruits and vegetables."

Huge pyramids of fragrant pineapples were mounded next to great fans of ripe bananas, oranges and limes. In addition, there were exotic offerings that Logan identified for her as the small, fuzzy kiwis and the strange-looking, leathery breadfruit, or paw paws as the natives called them.

Lisa was in seventh heaven as they strolled along, her bright head bobbing up and down next to Logan's broad shoulder. Suddenly the sky darkened. She looked up in surprise as the first big drop hit her tilted nose.

"How can it be raining when the sun was out just a minute ago?" she asked.

"Oh, oh, I'd forgotten about that!" Logan took off his jacket as the deluge started.

Wrapping her in his coat, he raced her across the street and up the rickety steps of a big wooden building. It took only a few moments, but they were both drenched by the time they reached the overhang.

"I can't believe this!" she marveled. "It's an absolute downpour!"

"That's the way it rains here." Logan pulled the jacket more closely around Lisa, looking at her anxiously. "Are you all right? I don't want you to catch a chill."

She laughed helplessly. "It's eighty degrees out."

"But you just got over a bad illness." Holding her in the curve of his arm, Logan gently brushed the wet hair out of her eyes.

They were standing very close together in the shadows and Lisa's hand moved irresistibly to his wet shirt front, feeling the steady beat of his heart. "You're the one who is soaked," she murmured.

Logan's fingers feathered her cheek, moving to the delicate skin behind her ear and tracing a path to the hollow of her throat where a pulse beat wildly. "I don't mind," he said softly.

She touched the dark hair that showed through the open neck of his sport shirt, feeling the warmth of his skin. Almost unconsciously she unfastened the next button and slid her hand inside, moving her palm over the hard-muscled chest. Her breathing was constricted as she whispered, "We ought to be getting back so you can get out of these wet clothes."

He drew her slowly closer and she raised her face to his. A flame leaped through Lisa's body as her lips parted in anticipation. They seemed cut off from the rest of the world, enclosed in a private place, an Eden all their own.

An aggrieved voice shattered the illusion. "Isn't this weather the pits?" Marsha was shaking her head vigorously to dislodge the raindrops.

For a moment Lisa found it difficult to return to reality, but Logan didn't seem to be affected. Moving casually away, he turned to the other woman. "We forgot rule number one—never go out in Pago Pago without an umbrella."

"I don't know if I'm an optimist or a fool, but I didn't believe it could rain so suddenly," Marsha said.

"Or clear up so fast," Logan said, pointing to the sunshine that had appeared like magic. "Come on, ladies, I'll get us a cab."

"I think I'll stay out and do a little shopping," Marsha told him. "The next rain isn't due for another hour. How about it, Lisa? Would you like to look around the stores?"

"That sounds like fun. You don't mind do you, Logan?" In a way, Lisa was glad to escape his dominating presence for a while. Their latest encounter was too fresh in her mind. It didn't seem to mean anything to Logan, but Lisa was still shaken.

"I think you should go back to the hotel and change." He frowned.

"Oh, Logan, don't be such a dictator," Marsha scoffed. "She'll dry off in five minutes once we get out in the sun."

When he gave in reluctantly, Lisa found herself breathing a sigh of relief. She wanted to drink in this tropical paradise, yet with Logan around, nothing seemed to matter except being close to him.

Lisa had known Marsha only casually, but she found the other woman easy to be with. As they wandered in and out of the small shops, she found herself relaxing and enjoying herself.

They bought avidly, like tourists anywhere—gaily decorated straw handbags, colorful beads and perfume made from the delicately scented frangipani blossoms. Marsha even bought a *tupenu,* a long, sarong-type garment, and talked Lisa into buying one too in a beautiful green and white print. By the time they started back to the hotel, they were both loaded down with packages.

Lisa turned to Marsha with a sigh of pure delight. "What fun that was! Poor Mrs. Livingstone, it's a good thing she doesn't know what she's missing."

"Rhoda?" Marsha raised her eyebrows. "She doesn't come on these junkets."

"You mean Logan just picks some lucky girl out of the steno pool?"

"Actually, this is the first time Logan has ever concerned himself with the preliminaries. We were all amazed when we discovered he was coming, especially since Rhoda isn't around to hold down the fort. What happened to her anyway?"

"Didn't you know? Her daughter is having a baby and Mrs. Livingstone asked for time off to be with her."

Marsha shook her head. "I don't believe it. Rhoda is so dedicated to Logan that she wouldn't ask for time off if *she* was having a baby. She even comes in on Saturdays sometimes without being asked."

The subject was forgotten when Chuck hailed them from the hotel driveway. "I see you two have been out shopping while the rest of us have been slaving away," he joked.

"The day you overwork is the day I'm elected President," Marsha scoffed.

"You just don't appreciate me." He put an arm around Lisa's shoulders. "Now this little doll would never say anything that unfeeling."

"She will when she knows you better. Hi, Logan," Marsha called to the man who appeared on the veranda steps.

"Uh, oh," Chuck muttered under his breath, removing his arm hurriedly.

Marsha started up the steps, saying over her shoulder, "Wear your *tupenu* tonight, Lisa. I'm going to wear mine."

Logan's amused glance took in the packages the two were laden with. "It looks like you bought out the town."

"Yes, it . . . it does, doesn't it? Wait for me, Marsha, I'm coming too," Lisa called breathlessly. She knew Logan had forgotten all about the little incident in town, but she still felt unaccountably shy about being alone with him.

Dinner was a gala affair. Their party filled two large candlelit tables in the long dining room that overlooked the water. The windows were open to the tropic breeze and the ocean formed a murmuring background to their conversation.

They were all assembled when Lisa arrived, rather diffident in her native attire. The long gown clung lovingly to her curves, and although her legs were covered, she was uncomfortably aware of the swell of her breasts over the low-cut neckline. Also, the yellow hibiscus she had tucked in her long hair had seemed like a good idea at the time, but she now felt a little self-conscious. Her reception, however, couldn't have been more enthusiastic.

"You look fantastic, Lisa," Chuck said, bounding out of his chair to kiss her on the cheek. The smell of liquor on his breath, plus his flushed face, indicated that he had been drinking more than was prudent.

The others were a little more restrained, yet equally enthusiastic.

"That gown is a perfect color for you," Vince said, with his artist's instinct. "It's the exact color of your eyes."

Lisa slipped into the chair next to Logan, looking up for his approbation. His opinion was the only one that really meant anything, but she was doomed to disappointment. He was regarding her with a frown.

"Don't you like it?" she asked hesitantly.

His answer was cool. "You look very nice."

"Oh, come on, Logan, admit she's gorgeous," Chuck said. "She looks like a genuine native."

Logan raised a sardonic eyebrow. "A red-haired native?"

"Okay, so it's a little poetic license," Chuck conceded. "In any color though, she's smashing." He snapped his fingers. "Hey, I've got an idea! How would you like to do a walk-on in the picture, Lisa?"

"Oh, Chuck, don't be ridiculous." She laughed.

"I'm not kidding. Why don't you give it a whirl?"

"It might be fun at that, Lisa," Marsha said.

"Sure, why not?" John Babcock joined in.

"Stick with me, baby. I'll put your name in lights," Chuck growled in a phony Humphrey Bogart accent.

Lisa gurgled with laughter. "It would serve you all right if I took you seriously."

"We are serious," Chuck told her. "How about it, Logan? Wouldn't it be a gas?"

Logan's eyes were cold as he looked around the table. "I think it's a lousy idea, but if that is what Lisa has her heart set on, far be it from me to stand in her way."

The merriment died abruptly. Lisa felt like a child who has just been rebuked, and she had a feeling the others felt that way too. "It was only a joke, Logan. Of course I wouldn't do it," she said soberly.

They all tried to recapture the gaiety of the evening, but a pall seemed to have been cast over dinner and it broke up early. When Lisa said a halting good night to Logan, he looked at her with disinterest.

She was brushing her hair the next morning when Logan tapped on the door. His dark mood of the night before had vanished.

Leaning against the door jamb, he looked impossibly handsome in tight, well-washed jeans and a navy T-shirt. There was a quizzical smile on his face. "Are you ready to go on tour?"

"What do you mean?" she asked warily.

"I promised to show you the island, didn't I?"

"Oh, but . . . you took me into town yesterday."

"That was just a teaser. Today we'll take a ride to the other side and stop for a swim. Would you like that?"

"It sounds wonderful! Are you sure you can take the time?"

"What's the point in being the boss if you can't do what you want once in a while?" He grinned. "Put your suit on under your clothes and I'll meet you in the lobby in five minutes."

It took her less than that. Logan was waiting beside a car drawn up to the entrance, and they were soon on their way through countryside of incredible beauty. There were flowers everywhere, growing wild as well as bordering neat little houses in the villages they passed through. The narrow road wound through wilderness at times before turning abruptly to parallel the ocean. It was as though the road had been laid out with the express purpose of showing off the many and varied aspects of the island.

On the other side was a picture-postcard beach. The broad strip of white sand was crescent-shaped, embracing a lagoon of calm blue water edged with lacy foam. People were sunbathing lazily while children spashed around in the sparkling surf. Farther out, sailboats skimmed the surface like large white birds.

Logan stopped the car, turning to Lisa with a smile. "A nice, secluded beach would have been more romantic, but as you noticed, there aren't any."

"I hadn't thought about it, yet now that you mention it, this is the first one I've seen."

"That's because these are coral islands," he explained. "There are only a few sand beaches so, unfortunately, they are heavily populated."

"I don't mind," Lisa said, avoiding the look in his eyes.

After choosing a spot away from everyone else, Logan spread out the towels, then casually stripped off his clothes. As he shrugged out of his T-shirt, Lisa's eyes were drawn to his powerful shoulders and the tanned chest darkened by crisp hair. She couldn't seem to look away when he pulled down the tight jeans, revealing narrow hips and long, muscular legs.

"Aren't you going swimming?"

Logan was regarding her questioningly, and Lisa drew a shuddering breath. "I . . . yes, of course."

She hurriedly pulled her cotton shirt over her head, thankful that it hid her face for a moment. Logan stretched out a hand to smooth her hair which had become ruffled in the process, his eyes lighting with a special glow.

"You look like a rose," he said. Taking in her slender body in the tiny suit that concealed very little, he added softly, "A beautiful red rose."

Lisa's heart was beating so fast she thought he must

surely hear it. "I'll race you to the water," she gasped, darting away without waiting to see if he was following.

Logan overtook her easily. Grasping her hand, he pulled her along after him into the foaming water. He was a strong swimmer and although Lisa managed to keep up with him, she had a feeling that he was tempering his pace to suit her own. He also sensed immediately when she was tiring, making the decision to go back.

After they dried off, Logan suggested a walk. They strolled far up the beach, passing all the little knots of people until they came to a spot that was virtually deserted. The sand was just a narrow spit here, becoming ever narrower as the incoming tide ate away at it.

"I guess this is the end of the road," Lisa said, turning to go back.

Logan put his hand on her arm. "There is no hurry. Let's sit here on the sand for a while."

His hand felt like it was burning his special brand into her skin. "But our towels are back there," she pointed out.

"So are crowds of people."

She laughed nervously. "Not crowds, surely. You make it sound like Coney Island in July."

"Even one person would be too many," he said impatiently.

"You are really spoiled, do you know that?" she commented lightly. "You're so used to private pools and private clubs and—"

His hand at the nape of her neck effectively silenced the desperate spate of words. With his eyes holding hers hypnotically, Logan's fingers moved sensuously over her skin, tangling in the damp curls and gently massaging her scalp. Pulling her closer to him, he brushed his lips over her cheek, murmuring in her ear. "You know why I don't want anyone else around."

Lisa felt the silken web of danger enfolding her, yet she didn't have the strength to move away. That hard, male body was seducing her until the thing she wanted most in life was to melt against him and feel his arms holding her tightly.

With a tremendous effort, she looked away from the flame in those burning blue eyes. "I think you've had a little too much sun," she said in an unsteady voice.

Surprisingly, he laughed. "Do you think the sight of you in those two ridiculous little scraps have inflamed my male lust?"

"Of course not!" Her cheeks colored to match the suit.

"I've seen you with even less, remember," he said softly.

How could he be cruel enough to remind her of that awful night? Jerking away from his caressing hands, Lisa faced him furiously. "And you managed to control yourself quite well, didn't you?" As soon as the words were out she was horrified. It sounded as though she was *complaining* because he had!

"Not because I wanted to, I assure you."

"Why are you dragging that all up now?" she cried.

"Because I want you." His hands were on her waist, drawing her gently closer. She quickly put her palms against his chest to hold him off. "Don't look so startled, little rosebud." He laughed. "I don't mean here. But I do want you."

The feel of his warm skin made her tremble and she caught her lower lip in her teeth. "When did you come to that conclusion?"

"I suppose the first time I saw you. Even though you looked like a little drowned kitten." He smiled.

"Please stop!" She caught at the hands that were smoothing her skin sensuously. "I don't understand any of this, Logan. You never acted like you . . . well . . . wanted me. Even when I . . ." she swallowed hard, "when I wasn't quite myself."

"You have a convenient memory. The way I recall it is that I was starting to make rather serious love to you."

"But you stopped," she said dully.

"Yes, unfortunately, I stopped."

"Why did you change your mind? I mean now," she added hastily. "What happened to all that talk about saving myself for someone I really love?"

A curtain seemed to drop in back of his eyes. "That was before I knew your views on marriage," he said smoothly.

She looked at him blankly. "What does that have to do with it?"

"Quite a lot. You see, Lisa, you are very innocent. Never having given yourself to a man, you don't know how very powerfully the act of love can affect you. It's very common for a girl to imagine herself madly in love with the first man she's been with. Especially an experienced man." His voice grew husky as he gently traced the shape of her mouth. "I can give you pleasure like you never dreamed of. I can light a fire in that beautiful body that will lift you like a rocket to the stars."

Her heart was thundering as his long fingers trailed sensuously down her throat and across the soft swell of her breasts above the bikini top. But along with the raging excitement was a burning anger.

"It's very kind of you to offer to initiate me," she said bitingly. "I'd be more impressed if it weren't done so cold-bloodedly." Her eyes flashed with dislike. "You could be outsmarting yourself, you know. If you can deliver all those earthly delights, what makes you think I wouldn't fall madly in love with you like any other silly innocent?"

He smiled mockingly. "I could live with that."

"Oh, sure! Just as long as I didn't want you to marry me," she said bitterly.

He looked at her sharply. "Have you changed your mind? You don't want to get married, do you?"

She raised her chin to keep it from trembling. "No! Certainly not! That's one thing you don't have to worry about."

A muscle worked in his jaw. "Then I don't see what you're angry about."

"You don't—!" She took a deep breath to steady

herself. "Let me put it this way—thank you for your kind offer, but I'm not interested."

Whirling around, she started swiftly up the beach. Logan overtook her with lazy strides. Looking straight ahead, she said stiffly, "I'll arrange to be on the first flight back home."

"Why on earth would you want to do a thing like that?"

At the amusement in his voice, she faced him incredulously. "I naturally assumed . . . I mean, you wouldn't want me around if—"

Logan chuckled. "Lisa, my little innocent, this isn't the end of the world. I propositioned you and you turned me down. It's no big deal." He shrugged.

"I don't suppose it's ever happened to you before," she said resentfully.

"Not often," he conceded. "But I'll survive."

"I'm sure there are any number of women who would be glad to oblige," she said, unable to leave it alone.

Her heart plunged like a stone when he agreed. "More than you know, little rosebud."

On the ride back to the hotel, Logan acted as though nothing had happened. It was an effort for Lisa to match his casual tone and she envied the way he managed it so easily. Of course his heart wasn't involved like hers was. For one treacherous moment she wondered why she didn't take him up on his offer. Wasn't a tiny bit of heaven better than none at all? Almost immediately Lisa realized that it would be followed by a hell too terrible to imagine. Loving him as she did, it would be almost impossible to keep from demanding more. And once he discovered the depth of her feeling for him and what her secret dreams were, he would put her out of his life completely.

Lisa sighed and looked out the window, blinking away hopeless tears. Unless she could reconcile herself to never seeing Logan again, she would have to make very sure to keep him at arm's length.

Chapter Five

Their stay on Pago Pago was all too brief for Lisa, although the yacht that Logan hired eased the pain of parting. It was a sleek white cruiser fitted out with every luxury, and Lisa found herself wishing the trip was longer than just overnight.

They spent the afternoon in deck chairs discussing the forthcoming film, pausing now and then to watch a school of flying fish soar in a graceful arc, or to have their glasses replenished by the competent steward.

Dinner that evening was a relaxed affair in the handsome dining room, after which they all moved to a large salon with comfortable couches and a standing card table and chairs. Some of the men played gin rummy while the others talked lazily to an accompaniment of soft stereo music. It was like a glamorous dream from which Lisa was sure she would awaken any moment.

Through the broad picture windows she could see the moon shining on the inky water, spreading a silver carpet it seemed almost possible to walk on. It drew her irresistibly and she quietly slipped away to enjoy the magic of the night.

The sky was peppered with millions of stars, some cold as diamond chips, others glowing like tiny embers. She was staring at them in rapt admiration when a deep voice broke into her reverie. "Are you all right?" Logan asked.

"Yes, of course."

His eyes were concerned. "You left without a word. I thought perhaps something was wrong."

She lifted her head once more, gazing up at the sky. "It's so beautiful out here, I just couldn't stay inside."

"Yes, it's very beautiful," he said softly, taking in the pure line of her throat.

"When you look up at all those millions of stars and realize how infinite the world is, it makes all your troubles seem insignificant, doesn't it?"

"Do you have troubles, Lisa?"

She gave a self-conscious little laugh. "Not really. Not compared to some people, I suppose."

"I wouldn't like to think that I was the cause of any of your troubles."

"You aren't." But she couldn't look at him.

"I wish you had said that with a little more conviction," he said wryly. "Was it what happened at the beach yesterday? Is that still bothering you?"

Lisa clasped the railing and looked down at the swirling water. "Maybe a little," she admitted.

He cupped her chin in his hand, gently turning her head so she had to look at him. "Then put it out of your mind. Let's just go back to being friends, shall we?"

She gave him a tremulous smile. "I'd like that."

"I would too. So that's what we'll be from now on."

He squeezed her hand briefly and Lisa gave a small sigh. Logan obviously found her easy to give up. She wished she could turn off her own emotions as easily.

The next morning everyone was up early for their arrival in Nuku'alofa, the capital city of Tonga. Once again, they entered a tropical paradise.

An ancient bus stood waiting at the dock, its sides gaily decorated with palm fronds and exotic red and yellow ginger blossoms. Its lack of windows was referred to with much hilarity as natural air conditioning. Nothing could have provided a more striking contrast to the luxury of the yacht, yet nobody seemed to mind.

When they got under way, Lisa stared out of the window, enchanted by the beauty of the island as well as by the tall, graceful people who greeted them with a wave and a flash of white teeth in handsome brown faces. "Where are we going, Logan?" she asked, scarcely able to tear her eyes from them.

He brushed away a long strand of auburn hair that had whipped across her face. "To look for romantic sites. Not an easy job at nine o'clock in the morning, is it?"

Lisa's heart gave a little lurch as she looked into the clear blue eyes smiling down at her. "Oh, I don't know. Anyone who can't get romantic in these islands, whatever the hour, isn't really trying," she said flippantly.

"You haven't demonstrated that ability," he said dryly.

She had brought that on herself, Lisa thought, flushing as she turned back to gaze out at the magnificent scenery. Soon a sight greeted her that banished any lingering embarrassment. A huge black stone arch stood like a brooding sentinel in the middle of a clearing. "What on earth is that?" she asked.

"It's called the Ha'amonga Stones, although actually, they're made from hardened coral."

"But what is it for?"

"It was built as a seasonal calendar," Logan explained. "And it could still serve that purpose if necessary. Lines carved on the lintel point directly to the rising sun on the longest and shortest days of the year."

They all piled out of the bus and went closer to inspect the impressive structure that their driver told them was built in the year 1200. It looked to Lisa like one of the inexplicable monuments she had seen pictured at Stonehenge in England. The wonder of it was how stones weighing many tons each had been erected without the use of modern equipment.

When the others fanned out to inspect the surrounding terrain, Lisa drifted toward the ocean, pausing to appreciate the aptly named flame trees covered with brilliant red blooms. Climbing down a low embankment, she had a breathtaking view of the island, like a low green crescent with leafy arms spread wide to embrace the sparkling blue water.

There wasn't a ship on the horizon or a plane in the sky. Lisa felt transported back in time to that earlier age when this lovely island was newly risen from the sea.

The sound of her name being called finally brought her back to reality. Turning reluctantly, she found Logan watching her. "I wondered where you had gotten to," he said, extending his hand to help her up the bank.

"I'm sorry. I guess I was so hypnotized by the view that I forgot about the time. Did you want me for something?"

"No, but we're ready to leave. I think we've wrung all of the information out of this place."

"Did you want me to take notes?" She indicated her capacious shoulder bag. "I brought along my notebook."

"That won't be necessary."

As he started to lead her toward the bus, Lisa hung back. "Logan, I haven't done a single lick of work since we arrived. Everyone here has a job to do except me." She looked up at him searchingly. "You didn't really need me, did you?"

His eyes got that hooded look Lisa hated because it meant she didn't know what he was thinking. "Why do you persist in making me altruistic when all of the evidence is to the contrary?"

"All right, then tell me what use I've been."

"The trip isn't over yet," he said smoothly. "I prefer to dictate everything at one time, after I've had a chance to mull it over in my mind."

She regarded him doubtfully. "When will that be?"

"When I tell you," he answered shortly. "If you are so concerned about pulling your weight, I suggest you stop making me waste time looking for you every five minutes."

Lisa followed him meekly back to the bus, aware that he was annoyed with her. But the nagging little doubts still nibbled away. Why had Logan brought her? If he needed a secretary, it hadn't been apparent so far.

They all trooped back in the bus and proceeded around the island, stopping when some location looked especially promising. Along the way they passed the *langi,* the ceremonial burial ground of ancient Tongan chieftains.

The tombs of the Tongan kings were huge quadrilateral mounds faced by tremendous blocks of coral, terraced to rise as much as twenty feet above the ground. Mounds of sand covered each grave, although there were no headstones to tell which mighty chief lay beneath.

"Time to get back to work," Logan called, herding them back on the bus. But when they passed an open-air market he relented.

"Look at all those beautiful baskets!" Lisa exclaimed. "And the children. Have you ever seen anything so adorable?"

A little girl in a brilliant red blouse, her pigtails tied with a blue ribbon to match her shorts, was smiling shyly at them. Spread out around her were slippers gaily decorated with straw flowers, braided hats and tapa cloths, those wall hangings hand blocked on parchment made from the paper mulberry tree. All along the road were examples of native crafts offered by dark-eyed, colorfully clad men and women.

Logan took one look at Lisa's wistful face and ordered the driver to stop once more. "I'm beginning to think I should have left you home after all," he teased, putting his arm around her to show he didn't mean it.

They were approaching the yacht when Ted said, "You don't need me any longer, do you, Logan? I was thinking maybe I'd catch the inter-island plane back to Pago Pago and take the night flight home. That way I can have these pictures developed by the time all of you return."

Everyone knew that Ted had only been married a month so he came in for some good-natured ribbing, but Logan looked thoughtful.

"That's a good idea, Ted. In fact, you can all go back and work up your reports. Lisa and I will return the yacht and catch the mid-morning flight."

There was a moment's silence before everyone started to talk at once.

Only Lisa was silent. The thought of being all alone on the yacht with Logan was an unexpected complication. She didn't want to be alone with him; more because she didn't trust herself than the other way around.

When they were back on board and the others were busily packing, she said tentatively, "Maybe I should go back with them, Logan."

"I thought you were complaining because you haven't done any work."

"But that's just it—I haven't."

"You will," he promised. "I want to dictate my impressions of both islands and the advantages and disadvantages of each."

"You mean tonight, on the way back to Pago Pago?"

"That's the general idea." He raised a sardonic eyebrow. "Unless you have something else in mind."

She colored a delicate pink. "No, of course not!"

"In that case, get out your notebook. I'll meet you up on deck as soon as everyone clears out."

Logan was as good as his word. They worked at top speed for several hours, his retentive memory spewing out details she had completely forgotten. He was concise, yet impartial, leaving Lisa completely in the dark as to his ultimate decision.

"I can't tell from this which location you've actually decided on," she said finally.

"I haven't. What would be the point in bringing the whole crew out here if I didn't wait for their input?"

"But you must have a preference. You could tell me," she coaxed.

"That would make quite a scoop for one of the movie columns," he said coolly.

Lisa looked at him with stricken eyes. "Do you really believe I would leak confidential information?"

Logan shook his head in annoyance at himself. "Of course not, Lisa. Forgive me."

He reached for her hand, but she drew back. "It's the truth. Why bother to deny it?"

"No, it isn't, I swear to you."

"You don't trust anyone, do you, Logan?" Lisa asked sadly. "Maybe that's the price one has to pay for getting where you are. Why only women though? Hasn't a man ever betrayed you?"

"I'll admit I'm cynical, Lisa; this business has made me that way. But you're wrong in thinking that I don't trust you." He jammed his hands in his pockets. "You've given me back my faith in human nature. Maybe I'm just afraid to believe it."

She stood up. "If you've finished, I'll transcribe these notes. I noticed a typewriter in the small salon."

His hand on her arm stopped her. "I thought we had agreed to be friends."

She gave him a level look. "I doubt if that's possible. You've never had a woman for a friend."

"There is always a first time." His mouth curved in a wry smile, but there was an enigmatic look in his eyes. "You already occupy a rather special place in my life."

As what? Lisa wondered. "Don't play games with me, Logan. I'm way out of my depth with you—" she waved her arm to encompass the yacht "—with this whole life you people live. I don't know what you want from me."

"Don't you?" he murmured. "I thought I was quite transparent."

She shook her head helplessly. "I don't understand you at all. Sometimes you treat me like a child, and other times—"

"Yes?" he prompted.

"And other times you don't," she finished lamely.

"Surely that isn't so difficult to understand. You're very beautiful, Lisa. I can't be the first man who has made a pass at you."

"You're the first one who runs hot and cold," she said bluntly.

The laugh lines around his eyes came into play. "I can assure you that I never feel cold toward you."

"Well, you act like it sometimes."

"When, for instance?"

"When . . . I don't now . . . yes, I do! When Chuck was joking about my doing a walk-on in the movie. You were really rotten about it."

The amusement disappeared from Logan's face. "You know how I feel about this business."

"About no-talent people, you mean. But how do you know I wouldn't turn out to be a great actress?"

Deep lines appeared around his mouth as Logan said harshly, "I didn't realize you were harboring a secret desire to be a movie star after all."

"I'm *not!* I only meant—oh, what's the use?" She stood up, clutching the notebook to her breast. "I'll type up these notes."

Logan let her go, his expression completely unreadable as he watched her slender figure disappear inside the salon.

The small cabin that housed the typewriter was warm, even though Lisa opened the sliding glass windows. Logan's observations were extensive, and by the time they were transcribed, she felt hot and sticky. Small beads of perspiration had reduced her hair to a mass of auburn ringlets.

She found Logan lying on a deck chair in the shade. He had changed into white shorts that showed off the deep tan of his broad chest and long, bare legs. He was working on a clipboard propped against his knees, a tall iced drink on the table next to him. In contrast to Lisa who felt hot and untidy, Logan looked cool and comfortable.

"Here are your notes," she said shortly.

"Thank you." He squinted into the sun, smiling as though there had been no unpleasantness between them. "You look like you've been in a sauna."

"It was hot inside," she said resentfully.

"I would have brought the typewriter out here."

"It doesn't matter, I'm through now. Unless you have something else for me?"

"Not at the moment. Why don't you get into your suit and join me? It's cool under the awning."

Lisa decided it would be childish to refuse. Besides, the brisk breeze off the ocean was irresistible. After a refreshing shower, she put on a pair of brief yellow shorts and a matching halter top.

A deck chair had been placed next to Logan's, with a tall, frosted glass on the table next to it. "I ordered you some lemonade," he said. "Is that all right?"

"Perfect," she said gratefully, bending down to pick up the drink. "Ouch!" In her haste to get back on deck, Lisa had caught her long hair in the ties of the halter top.

"What's the matter?"

She winced as the tangled strands resisted her efforts to free them. "I'm caught."

"Here, let me." A casual arm around her middle pulled her down onto his chaise. Lisa quivered, sitting up straight as her back came in momentary contact with his bare chest, but his arm continued to encircle her waist. "Don't squirm or I can't help you."

"It's all right, I can do it," she protested weakly, afraid that Logan could actually feel the thrills running through her body.

"Hold your hair out of the way," he said impatiently. When she unwillingly piled the shining mass on top of her head, he clucked his tongue. "Well, no wonder. You've got it all knotted."

It seemed to take forever to untie the knot she had tightened inadvertently. Logan's long fingers worked at it patiently, his feathery touches at the nape of her neck bringing both agony and ecstasy.

"Aren't you through yet?" she cried finally, unable to bear the sensuous feel of his hands on her.

"If you'd stop wiggling—ah, there, I've got it."

The strings were finally untied and Logan freed the tangled strands, his fingers combing gently through her hair. Weakness enveloped Lisa as his hands descended to her shoulders, massaging them gently before spreading sensuously over her back. Unable to stop herself, she leaned against him, giving in completely to the rapture he could awaken so easily. But when his warm lips touched the nape of her neck, an electric shock ran through her. She straightened hurriedly, clutching at the halter top.

"That was my reward for extricating you." Logan chuckled, gathering the strings together and tying them in a neat bow.

"I could have done it myself," she answered in a strangled voice.

"Wasn't it more fun this way?" There was amusement in his eyes as he surveyed her flushed face. "Lie down and cool off, Lisa."

She did as he said, pointedly picking up a paperback book she had brought along. Logan's chuckle wasn't lost on her, but he made no further comment, settling back with his clipboard.

The sun was dipping into the water, painting the sky a medley of rose tints, when he stood up and stretched. "I think I'll go put some clothes on."

Lisa consulted her watch. "I guess it is getting toward dinnertime."

"Would you like to have it here on deck?"

"Oh, Logan, could we? That would be lovely."

"I'll go tell the steward. Meet you back here in a little while."

When Lisa returned after changing to a filmy cotton print, darkness had fallen in the swift way it occurred in the tropics. The sky was sequined with stars that winked back at the flickering candles illuminating the white draped table set up on deck. Crystal wineglasses sparkled in the light that also illuminated the centerpiece of exotic flowers.

"It's so beautiful I feel like I'm part of an illustration in a brochure!" she exclaimed.

"You could very well be," Logan said huskily, coming out of the shadows. His white slacks were topped by a black silk shirt, unbuttoned almost to the waist. Turning toward a small bar that had been set up, he asked, "What can I fix you to drink?"

"Anything," she murmured, adding hastily, "as long as it's not too strong."

"Don't worry." He grinned. "I know your capacity." The candlelight revealed her blush and he mercifully changed the subject. "Tell me, what is your impression of the South Sea islands?"

"They're simply marvelous, so peaceful and unspoiled."

"Progress—and I use the term advisedly—is catching up with them, though. You should have seen Pago Pago in the days before jets."

"You've been here before?"

He nodded. "Some time ago."

She looked at him uncertainly. "Then why did you come on this trip, Logan? Everyone was surprised. They said you've never scouted locations before."

There was a mocking lift to his firm mouth. "Maybe I thought the romance of the tropics would inflame your blood and you'd fling yourself into my arms."

Lisa's long eyelashes swept her flushed cheeks. "I asked you a serious question."

His dark brows peaked in derision. "And you think I'm not serious?" When she shifted uneasily he said, "All right, emerald eyes, I won't tease you anymore. Maybe part of it was a hankering to climb out of my ivory tower for a while. I enjoyed our sightseeing trips even if you didn't. Your fresh enthusiasm made everything seem new."

"I never said I didn't enjoy it," she protested.

"All of it?" The candlelight made little flames in his eyes.

Lisa pleated her napkin nervously, knowing he was referring to the incident on the beach. When she didn't answer, Logan sighed. "There was another reason for this trip, of course. It's been so long since I was here that I wanted to be sure the islands were still reasonably unspoiled. Fortunately, there are some things even progress can't change—the magnificent harbor entrance to Pago Pago, for instance. That's really why I elected to take the yacht back instead of flying home with the others. To see it again."

The simple explanation sounded a death knell to any romantic dreams Lisa might still be cherishing. It was stupid and illogical, yet in the deep recesses of her heart, she hoped Logan had chosen to sail back in order to be alone with her.

Taking a deep breath she said brightly, "I can't wait to see it from a ship either."

"You'll have to get up early in the morning then. The captain tells me we round the first bend soon after seven."

"I wouldn't miss it for anything," she assured him. "Do you have an alarm clock you can lend me?"

"Wouldn't you rather be awakened like Sleeping Beauty?" he teased. When her apprehensive eyes flew to his face he took her hand, kissing the palm. "Don't panic, rosebud, I'll scare up an alarm clock for you."

After dinner they strolled around the deck, pausing at the railing to watch the phosphorescent waves play leapfrog across the inky ocean. The evening flew by on enchanted wings, much too swiftly for Lisa, who would have liked it to go on forever. It was Logan who finally called a halt.

Running massaging fingers over the back of his neck, he sighed. "I don't suppose I can put off those stockholder reports any longer. I brought them with me from Los Angeles and I haven't looked at them since."

"Is there anything I can help you with?"

"No, this is one-man torture." He smiled.

"Well . . . I'll leave you then."

"Good night, Lisa," he said pleasantly.

She had undressed and put on a sleep teddy, something the saleslady had assured her was the latest thing. It was a tiny scrap of candlelight satin, the brief legs as well as the bosom trimmed with deep insets of lace. The front closed —barely—with a thin satin ribbon that matched the narrow ones over the shoulder. It was a frivolous, expensive little garment that Lisa had been unable to resist, assuaging her conscience with the excuse that the teddy would be cool in the tropics.

She had just finished brushing her hair when there was a knock on the door. Casting a quick glance at her scantily clad body, she called, "Who . . . who is it?"

"It's Logan. I have your alarm clock."

She glanced despairingly around for something to put on, finding nothing. Her robe was already packed at the bottom of her suitcase, as was everything else except the suit she would travel home in tomorrow. Not knowing what else to do, she opened the door a crack and stuck her bare arm out blindly.

Logan pushed the door open. "I have to show you how to work this thing, Lisa. I got it from one of the crewmen and he says—" The words came to an abrupt halt as he saw her for the first time. His eyes turned a smoky blue, traveling slowly down the enticing figure revealed so provocatively. "I must say that's an improvement over my pajama top."

Her hands nervously smoothed the satin over her slim thighs. "I didn't have . . . that is . . . oh, just give me the alarm clock and go!"

He moved toward her and Lisa caught her breath, her lips parting unconsciously at the sheer male magnetism he radiated. A flickering light made his eyes brilliant. "That's not what you really want, Lisa. Admit it."

"No! I mean, yes, it is!" she gasped.

He was towering over her now, enveloping her in the potent aura of masculinity that emanated from that powerful body. His fingers touched her petal-soft cheek, trailing down to trace the trembling mouth. Her senses drank in everything about him and cried for more, the warmth of his body, the gentleness of his hands.

Long fingers toyed with the satin bow between her breasts, slowly untying it while his eyes held hers hypnotically. "Tell me that you don't want me and I'll leave."

The neckline was open now almost to the waist and Logan's hand slipped inside, cupping the fullness of one breast, his thumb making a slow circle on the rosy tip. A long shudder ran through Lisa. "Oh, Logan," she sighed.

Gathering her in his arms he gave a low, throaty cry of triumph as his mouth captured hers. Lisa surrendered mindlessly, knowing only that she could no longer deny either of them. Her arms went around his neck and she ran her fingers lovingly through his thick hair. At her surrender, Logan groaned, molding her willing body to his hard length and burying his face in her neck.

He claimed her mouth again, lifting her in his arms and carrying her to the bed. Sinking down beside her without relinquishing her lips, he fondled her body with sensual caresses, lingering over the places that gave her the most pleasure. Lisa quivered under the long, drugging kisses, her body on fire with delight.

His mouth trailed over the white skin her bikini had preserved from the sun. "You have such a beautiful body, my darling. I want to touch every inch of you."

"I know," she murmured, sliding her hand inside his shirt. She, too, wanted to explore every part of him. Lisa felt a ripple of emotion go through him at her feathery caresses.

"I *need* you, Lisa," Logan said harshly, tangling his hands in her bright hair to immobilize her face for his suddenly savage kiss. "Don't ever leave me!"

Her drugged senses took a minute to register the hoarse cry. Surely he didn't mean that? It was only the passion of the moment that made him say something he didn't really feel. She was so inexperienced. Was this what all men said when they were making love?

Sensing her sudden tension, Logan lifted his head. Their eyes met. A curtain descended behind his as he smiled, a sardonic smile that chilled her. "Don't get excited, I'm not asking for a commitment from you."

Her aching body longed for him, but Lisa's mind couldn't accept this latest rejection. How could he make such passionate love to her and still hold back part of himself? "Don't worry," she said bitterly. "I don't have any long-term plans where you're concerned."

A look that she would have called pain, if she hadn't known better, crossed his face. "It doesn't matter, Lisa. Let me be the first. Let me teach you about love and then maybe—"

His mouth captured hers, probing with a masculine expertise that left her senses reeling. She struggled against the flames that threatened to engulf her as he transferred his warm lips to the delicate cord in her neck, nibbling his way to her earlobe which he nipped delicately.

His experience was too extensive and her love for him too great. It was a huge temptation to give in to him, yet Lisa knew that her torment would be even greater if she allowed him to initiate her into an ecstasy she could only guess at. How could she ever sleep alone after she knew what it was like to lie in the arms of the only man she would ever love? The taste he had given her was too heady. The complete knowledge would destroy her.

Summoning strength from an unknown source, Lisa dragged herself out of Logan's arms. "It's no good, Logan. We'd be getting too involved and neither of us wants a commitment. You said you would leave if I told you I didn't want you." She bent her head to hide the unbearable torture in her jade green eyes. "All right, I'll say it. I don't want you."

She heard his sharply indrawn breath, yet it barely penetrated the misery that enveloped her. Every quiver-

ing inch of her unfulfilled body reproached her more than
he ever could. But Logan didn't utter a word. Perhaps he
didn't trust himself to. There was controlled fury in the
way he propelled himself off the bed.

When he strode decisively out of the room, part of her
died. Lisa had to bite down hard on her knuckles to keep
from begging him to come back.

Chapter Six

Lisa gazed pensively out of her office window without really seeing the scene below. The fact that she was still working at Magnum Studios continued to amaze her. After that traumatic night on the yacht, she had never expected to see Logan again once they returned to Los Angeles. Just facing him the next day had been a nightmare!

Lisa had never considered herself a coward, yet the mere thought of having to accompany Logan on that long plane ride had reduced her to a quivering mass of nerves. What terrible things would he say to her? Knowing that she deserved them wasn't any comfort.

Logan, however, had confounded her as always. While he couldn't by any stretch of the imagination be called friendly, his manner was polite. There were none of the recriminations she expected, no biting sarcasm—and no interest. Stealing glances at his strong profile, Lisa could almost believe she had imagined the passion that had glowed in those startling blue eyes. They were cold and shuttered now, hiding his thoughts from the world.

His indifferent manner toward her reinforced the painful knowledge that she meant nothing to Logan. He was annoyed of course. She had hurt his macho pride, Lisa thought bitterly. But that's all it was. The fact that they would never see each other again wouldn't bother Logan. Maybe in time it wouldn't bother her either, Lisa hoped forlornly.

When he dropped her at her apartment she tried to force a smile. "Good-bye, Logan, and . . . thanks for everything."

"Good-bye, Lisa. Get some rest and don't come in till noon tomorrow."

Once more he had caught her off balance! She looked at his austere face for some sign that he was joking. There was none. "But you . . . I . . . surely you don't want . . ."

He cut into her halting words. "I want a secretary who is rested enough to function properly. You're no good to me unless you can. Now, if you don't mind, I'd like to get home too."

She put a restraining hand on his arm. "Logan, I can't come back to work for you as if nothing ever happened."

A wintry smile touched his firm mouth. "Nothing *ever* happens between us, Lisa."

"You know what I mean," she said in a choked voice.

His eyes were hard. "No, I'm afraid I never do."

"Logan, I—"

"You agreed to fill in until Mrs. Livingstone came back. I can't believe you're going to add undependability to your other . . . inadequacies. Just see that you're at your desk by noon. I imagine there is a lot of work backed up."

Under the circumstances Lisa had no choice, but she consoled herself with the thought that her sentence was almost up. Mrs. Livingstone was due back in a week. That escape hole was plugged a few days later when Rhoda telephoned with bad news. There had been complications with the baby and her daughter was back in the hospital. Mrs. Livingstone wouldn't be back for at least two more weeks, maybe three.

"When Mr. Marshall told me to take a leave of absence

I felt guilty," she confided over the phone. "Now I'm glad he insisted."

Lisa was slightly puzzled. Logan told her it was Mrs. Livingstone who had asked for the time off, yet she was indicating it was his idea. Marsha Block had said something to the same effect. But Lisa was too upset by the idea of having to stay longer to give it much thought. True, Logan wasn't giving her any trouble—maybe that was the problem. It was torture to be around him every day and be treated like a useful piece of furniture.

Another thing that troubled Lisa was the fact that she hadn't been able to pay Logan back any of the money he had spent on nurses. He was giving her a handsome salary, but so far it had all gone toward the bills that had accumulated while she was sick. She wanted to assure him that she hadn't forgotten about the debt; however, there didn't seem much point until she could pay him something. He wasn't that approachable anyway. Their only conversation was about business.

It was a lonely time for Lisa. She had been in Los Angeles for such a short time that she hadn't made any friends. Although she had acquaintances at the studio, that's all they were. Even the men who had initially expressed an interest in her no longer did so.

One Friday night after work, Lisa decided to do some necessary marketing—a task she wasn't too fond of. The supermarket was crowded, making shopping even more of a chore. By the time she wheeled her loaded cart to the check-out stand she was thoroughly dispirited.

Her purchases filled two large bags that she juggled uncomfortably as she rummaged for car keys that proved maddeningly elusive.

"Oh, no!" Lisa exclaimed suddenly, peering into the Morris Minor. She had locked her keys in the car!

"I beg your pardon?" A tall man with sun-streaked blond hair paused in the act of opening the door of a Cadillac parked next to the Morris. "Were you talking to me?"

"No, I was talking to myself—or maybe to God. He's the only one who can help me," Lisa muttered, scowling at the inoffensive little car.

"What seems to be the trouble?"

"I locked my keys in the car."

"Well, maybe I can help you." A smile lit his brown eyes. "It seems a shame to bother God with such a small problem."

"You aren't going to break a window, are you?" Lisa asked anxiously.

"Nothing so drastic." He reached into the rear of his car, taking a camel's hair jacket off its hanger and tossing it on the seat. "Luckily, I just picked up my cleaning."

She watched curiously as he straightened the hanger until it was a line of wire with a small curve at one end like a fish hook. "What are you going to do?" she asked.

"A little trick known to car thieves and law-abiding folk as well." He forced the wire between the window and the rubber strip that protected the door, maneuvering it until the hook was over the lock. Catching the pushed-down button in the curve, he gave a sharp upward tug and the button popped up. Opening the car door, he swept Lisa a mock bow. "Your chariot, milady."

"That was fantastic! I'll have to remember that." Her green eyes sparkled. "How can I ever thank you?"

He smiled at her animated face. "You could have a drink with me."

"Oh . . . I . . . I'm sorry, but—"

"You don't know me," he finished for her. "And you're a very proper young lady who doesn't allow strange men to pick her up."

"You make it sound very stuffy, but that's essentially correct." She smiled.

"Let me introduce myself, then we won't be strangers. I'm Bruce Devereaux, thirty-seven, unmarried, and very well-liked by dogs and children. I am also gainfully employed, although I do sneak off to go surfing whenever possible. I am an independent producer, currently finishing a movie and about to start a television show."

"Are you really?" Lisa exclaimed. "I'm in movies too."

He looked at her more closely. "You are? I'm sure I would have remembered that face. What have you done?"

"I'm not really *in* movies." She laughed. "I meant I work at Magnum Studios."

"What do you do? No, this is ridiculous," he interrupted himself. "We can't stand here in the parking lot. Let's go have one drink in there." He indicated a small bar in the shopping center. "Nothing can happen in a public place and you're free to go whenever you like. It's the same as standing here talking except that we'll be sitting down."

It seemed reasonable so Lisa allowed herself to be persuaded. Besides, he seemed very pleasant and he *had* done her a great service.

When they were seated in a comfortable booth, Bruce asked again, "What do you do at Magnum? And by the way, you haven't told me your name."

"It's Lisa Brooks, and I work for Logan Marshall."

"Doesn't everybody," was his wry comment. "Doing what?"

"I'm filling in for his private secretary while she's on vacation. It's a temporary job really."

"That's fortunate. Nobody should be sentenced to life with the tyrant of the tower."

"You know Logan?" When he nodded, Lisa said, "It doesn't sound as though you like him."

Bruce shrugged. "We've tangled a few times. Logan likes to rule with an iron hand, but I don't work for him so he can't tell me what to do."

Even though the description was fairly accurate, Lisa felt called upon to present a defense. "He has always been very kind to me." *For the most part,* she added silently.

Bruce's eyes wandered over her cynically. "I'm sure of that."

"Not in the way you are suggesting," Lisa said stiffly. "Logan and I are just friends."

He didn't bother to conceal his disbelief. "Are we talking about the same man? The Logan Marshall I know has always wanted just one thing from a woman as beautiful as you—and it isn't friendship."

Although it was what she had accused Logan of, Lisa's anger stirred. "Nevertheless, it's true. Our relationship is strictly platonic."

"Okay, if you say so. I think he's crazy, but I'm delighted to hear it." Bruce gave her a mischievous smile. "Logan is a mean adversary. I might think twice about trying to snatch one of his women out from under his nose."

Lisa looked at him with distaste. "I'm not 'one of his women,' nor am I up for grabs. I think I'd better be going. Thank you for your help this evening, Mr. Devereaux."

He put his hand on her arm as she started to rise. "I didn't mean to be insulting, Lisa. I'm really a very nice fellow who would like to get to know you better. You're different from most of the girls in this town."

"Couldn't you do better than that stale old line?" she asked scornfully.

"What can I do to convince you? Didn't I leap to your aid like Galahad on a white charger? I even tossed my one hundred percent camel's hair jacket in a heap on the back seat just for you. Doesn't that prove I'm a gentleman?"

An unwilling smile curved her lips. "No, it proves you're untidy."

"All right, so I'm a slob, but I'm a nice one. Tell me you'll go out with me."

"Maybe sometime," she said evasively.

He sighed. "I can see you're going to take a lot of convincing."

"Give it up, Bruce, you would just be wasting your time. I really *am* different from most of the women in this town. I'm not interested in a part in your upcoming epic, if that's the next thing you're going to offer. And I wouldn't go to bed with you even if I knew you better," she told him bluntly.

"I believe you're serious," he said slowly.

"I know it's hard to believe," she said dryly. "But look at all the wasted effort I saved you."

He looked at her searchingly. "I've never met anyone like you, Lisa—and in spite of what you think, that's no line. Can we at least be friends?"

She regarded him skeptically. "Our definition of the word is apt to differ."

"You're wrong," he said firmly. "I want to see you again on your own terms—nothing romantic, I promise you. How about a game of tennis tomorrow?"

At first Lisa refused, her objections crumbling when Bruce suggested she meet him at the courts. If she arrived and left in her own car, it wasn't a real date, was it? Perhaps the fact that she was tired of being alone so much was the final clincher.

To her surprise, the afternoon was a great success. Bruce was a good player, besides being a great deal of fun. After the game they had lunch at the tennis club he belonged to, and he regaled her with outrageous stories about people in the movie industry. When he asked her to take a ride to Malibu for lunch the next day, Lisa accepted without hesitation.

It was a sparkling Sunday afternoon, tailor-made for a drive to the beach. Lisa had never been to Malibu, that fabled retreat of the rich and famous, and she was looking forward to it.

They stopped at an excellent seafood restaurant just off the highway, where the food turned out to be superb. Bruce was charming. He seemed to have accepted the fact that she was only interested in friendship, never stepping over the line either by word or action.

When they were leaving the restaurant after lunch, he said, "A friend of mine has a rather unique house in the compound. It's all redwood and glass with a pretty spectacular view. Would you like to stop by and see it?"

The compound was a private area of expensive and interesting-looking homes, guarded by a gatehouse with an attendant. The Pacific Ocean was their front yard, all the houses turning their backs to the highway above.

"I'd like very much to see it, but shouldn't we call first?" Lisa asked.

"It isn't necessary. People drift in and out all day. You never know who you're going to see there."

It was only a short drive from the restaurant. When they arrived a few minutes later, Bruce opened the door without bothering to ring the bell. Once they were inside Lisa understood why. No one would have heard it anyway. The big living room that ran the width of the house was filled with people, all talking over the noise of the stereo. Almost all the guests had a glass in one hand as they stood around in groups, ignoring the magnificent view just beyond the wide picture windows.

"Which one is the host?" Lisa asked.

"Come on, I'll introduce you." Leading her over to a short, curly-haired man in tight jeans and sandals, Bruce said, "Meet Rudy Mandell, the best cameraman in the business."

After he had acknowledged the introduction, Rudy said to Bruce, "At last you brought me one I don't have to shoot through filters and baby spots." He took Lisa's chin in his hand, turning her head back and forth. "Exquisite! She doesn't have any bad angles."

Bruce laughed at the bewildered expression on Lisa's face. Putting his arm protectively around her, he said, "Sorry to disappoint you, pal, she isn't an actress."

"What are you talking about, she has a perfect face." Rudy's eyes swept over her. "The rest of her is pretty spectacular too."

Lisa's cheeks were pink with embarrassment. "Thank you, Mr. Mandell. The only problem is that I don't know how to act."

"Since when has that stopped anyone?" He snorted. "Oh, I get it, you're a model."

"No, I'm a secretary."

"She works for Logan Marshall," Bruce said significantly. The two men exchanged glances.

"Oh, I see," Rudy murmured.

No you don't see! Lisa wanted to shout. What good would it do though? These people had such tacky little minds. If a woman worked for a man, she was automatically sleeping with him. Lisa was beginning to be sorry she had come.

"I hope you know what you're doing, man," Rudy murmured cryptically, almost too low for Lisa to hear. Taking Bruce by the arm, he turned to Lisa and said, "Would you excuse us for a few minutes?"

She wandered over to the window where she could look at the view and not have to talk to anyone. There was a couple in the corner she was heading for, but it couldn't be helped. There was no totally secluded spot in this crowded room.

The woman facing her was a movie star of some magnitude, a sex symbol said to be much sought after. At the moment, however, she seemed to be the one doing the chasing. Her voice was lowered to a sexy pitch, while her hand gently stroked the sleeve of the man who towered over her.

Curious in spite of herself, Lisa looked to see who he was. Her heart gave a sudden lurch as the man turned out to be Logan! His back was to her, yet surely there was no mistaking that well-shaped head above those wide shoulders. Or was she doomed to see a resemblance in every tall, handsome man she ran across?

Lisa reached for the windowsill to steady herself, a mist of tears obscuring her view of the glass that sat on the ledge. It fell with a clatter. Luckily it was plastic, and the only damage was a small puddle on the hardwood floor. The clatter attracted Logan's attention.

"Can I do some—" The polite words were cut off abruptly. "Lisa! What are you doing here?"

Taking a deep breath, she smiled brightly. "The same thing you are, I imagine."

"I didn't know you knew Mandell. Where did you meet him?" He scowled.

"Right over in that corner," she said, answering his question literally.

"I mean to have the truth, Lisa." His dark brows were tightly drawn together.

"Logan!" His companion recalled his attention sharply.

He looked at her for a moment as though he had never seen her before. Then his poise returned. "Excuse me, my dear. Monica Miles, this is Lisa Brooks."

After a polite acknowledgment on both sides, the woman looked from Lisa to Logan. "One of your new little starlets, darling?" There was something unpleasant about her smile.

"As a matter of fact, Lisa is my secretary," Logan informed her smoothly.

Monica's eyebrows rose speculatively. Before she could comment, a man materialized at her side. "Monica, darling, I've been trying to tell that delicious story of yours about that would-be director, Zippoli, and I can't get it right. You'll have to do it." The man's arm around her shoulders urged her toward a group at the other end of the room, leaving her no option.

"I'm waiting for an explanation, Lisa," Logan's angry voice reminded her as soon as they were alone.

"I don't have to explain anything to you," she flared.

"You know I don't want you around these people."

"But it's all right for you, is that it?"

He controlled himself with an effort. "This is my business. I have to go a lot of places I wouldn't choose and associate with people who wouldn't be my first choice either."

"Poor thing!" Lisa's voice was heavy with sarcasm.

"That little tête-à-tête with Monica Miles must have been dreadful for you. I'll bet you could hardly bear the way she was stroking your sleeve!"

Something glinted in his eyes and the frown disappeared. "Jealous, Lisa?" he asked softly.

She drew in her breath sharply. "Certainly not! Why should I care who your latest woman is?"

"Why indeed?" he murmured. "Yet for a moment there, your eyes were remarkably green."

"They are *always* green—or haven't you noticed?"

"There isn't anything about you I haven't noticed." He smiled sardonically. "Don't forget, I've put you to bed more than once."

"Ohh!" Her breath was expelled in an outraged gasp. "You're detestable!" She turned away, but his firm grasp on her upper arm stopped her flight.

"Not so fast. You haven't told me how you got here."

"It's none of your business," she said mutinously.

"I've made it my business." There was a steely quality about him that warned Lisa he intended to have an explanation.

"I don't know what difference it makes to you," she cried in frustration. "You haven't shown any interest in how I spend my time until now. As long as I was moping around the house by myself, that was all right, is that it? Well, I got tired of being alone."

Logan's hard grip loosened. His fingers began to make little caressing motions on the soft skin of her inner arm. "Poor Lisa, have you been lonely?"

The sensuous feel of those long fingers on her skin was making her tremble. Jerking her arm away she glared at him. "Not for you, if that's what you're thinking."

Without either of them noticing his approach, Bruce joined them, draping his arm casually over Lisa's shoulders. "Sorry, love. Rudy always has some piece of business that can't wait."

Bruce's appearance couldn't have come at a more

opportune time. Lisa gazed up with an adoring look that made him blink. "That's all right, I understand," she said throatily.

If Bruce noticed the tension between the two, he gave no indication. Squeezing Lisa's shoulder, he said easily, "Hi, Logan, good to see you again."

Logan's frosty glance rested on the encircling arm. "I didn't know you knew my secretary, Devereaux."

"You might say I broke into her life." Bruce grinned.

"Where did you two meet?" Logan asked evenly.

"In the parking lot of the Safeway market," Lisa answered deliberately, knowing it would get a reaction.

Logan didn't disappoint her. His mouth curved contemptuously. "The cut-rate one?"

"Don't you think that's a little insulting, old man?" Bruce seemed unruffled, yet from the way his hand tightened on her shoulder, Lisa knew he wasn't as calm as he sounded. "You and I have had our run-ins in the past, but that's no reason to be offensive."

"I know your reputation with women, Devereaux."

Bruce gave a sharp laugh. "Coming from the stud of the Western world, that's very funny."

"I'm not interested in your opinion of my morals. I'm telling you to stay away from Lisa. She isn't your type."

"Then you have nothing to worry about, do you?" Bruce smiled infuriatingly.

"I'm warning you, Devereaux." Logan's nostrils flared in anger.

"That you'll do what? You can't threaten me, Logan. I don't work for you. I'm not one of your lackeys who quakes in his boots when you raise an eyebrow." Bruce's anger matched Logan's now, all pretense of indifference gone.

"Nevertheless, you'll stay away from her."

"Only when I hear it from the lady herself—and so far she hasn't made any complaints," Bruce added insinuatingly.

"Why you—!" Logan gripped a handful of the other man's shirt, jerking him so close that their faces were only inches apart.

Lisa had been trying to make herself heard for some time, to no avail. When she noticed the curious looks being cast in their direction, her heart sank. They were both well-known men. If they got into a fight over her, it might very well make the tabloids.

Insinuating herself between them, she tried to push them apart. "Stop it this minute, you two. I won't be fought over like some disgusting bone."

For a moment it seemed that she wouldn't be successful. Then the two men drew slowly apart, both breathing heavily.

"I want to go home," Lisa told Bruce, her eyes stormy pools of green.

"I'm sorry, honey, I guess this thing did get a little out of hand." Bruce's smile was tentative.

Logan didn't bother to try and placate her. His frown showed his continuing displeasure. "Lisa—"

"Don't say it, Logan," she warned. "Don't say *anything!* I don't think I could take much more."

Turning sharply, she walked through the crowded room with her head held high, trying to ignore the avid glances that raked her. Bruce trailed docilely in her wake. For his part, Logan watched them go, his eyes narrowed dangerously.

Chapter Seven

By Monday morning, Lisa was a bundle of nerves. Although she still resented the scene Logan had precipitated, her own anger had cooled somewhat, but she knew Logan was probably furious at the way she had walked out on him. Lisa dreaded the scene that would ensue.

Her fears on that score were groundless. For one thing, she didn't even see him until after lunch. Logan was closeted in a meeting to which she wasn't invited; he didn't call on her services until the afternoon.

Her nervousness when she walked into his office, clutching her steno pad, wasn't alleviated by the formidable expression on his face.

Without any reference to the unpleasantness that had marked their last meeting, he said, "I'm sending memos to the whole crew of the new movie. These instructions are very important, so be sure you get them right."

Lisa's head lifted sharply in a protest Logan didn't allow her to voice. As he launched immediately into rapid speech, his dictation had the crisp staccato of a machine gun. By dint of great concentration, she was able to keep up until Logan moved to the window where he gazed out over his domain without slackening the torrential spate of words.

"I'm sorry, I didn't get that last sentence. Would you repeat it?" she was forced to ask.

He turned toward her with a wolfish smile. "What happened to those vaunted secretarial skills of yours, Miss Brooks? Were your thoughts on your active social life?"

She held onto her temper with an effort. "Not at all, *Mr.* Marshall. It's just that most employers have the courtesy to face someone when they're dictating."

He sauntered lazily over until he was so close that his thigh almost brushed her arm. "Is this better?"

It was a great deal worse! As always, being in close proximity to Logan brought a reaction. This time it was nervousness so intense that she dropped her pencil. They both reached for it at the same time. When their fingers touched, Lisa jerked her hand away as though it had been burned.

"You seem remarkably jumpy this morning," Logan commented sardonically. "Is anything wrong?"

Everything is wrong, she wanted to shout! What had happened to the warm relationship they used to share? Where was the man who had been so tenderly concerned about her at one time? Lisa bent her head without answering, the shining curtain of long auburn hair hiding the tears that threatened.

"Lisa?" Logan's hand lifted her unwilling chin. "*Is* anything wrong?" The question was repeated in an entirely different tone of voice, seriously this time.

The mockery was gone from those startling blue eyes. It was a glimpse of the old Logan, and Lisa's parted lips trembled as she gazed up at him. He drew in a sharp breath, his fingers tightening on her chin. The peremptory shrill of the telephone ringing cut across whatever he had been about to say.

It was his private line so Lisa gathered up her notebook. "I'll type up these memos right away," she said, starting for the door.

Logan seemed about to say something, then thought

better of it. He let her go, staring after her slender figure with an inexplicable expression on his face.

With all the work that Logan had given her, it was a busy day. There was no time for any further conversation with him, which was another blessing. The way things were between them now, it could only end in disaster.

Bruce called that evening almost as soon as Lisa walked in the door. "Well, how did it go today?" he asked. "Are you still working at Magnum?"

"Of course," she answered shortly. "Why shouldn't I be?"

"After that little fiasco yesterday, I wasn't sure. I'm really sorry, Lisa. I didn't realize Logan would get so steamed about your being with me."

"He had no right to," she cried.

There was a slight hesitation before Bruce said, "If you say so."

"What is that supposed to mean?" she demanded. "I suppose you're still convinced that Logan and I are having an affair."

"I didn't say that," he protested.

"You didn't have to," Lisa said wearily. "If you don't mind, I'd rather not talk about it anymore."

"Right. That wasn't what I called for anyway. When am I going to see you again?"

"You mean yesterday didn't scare you off?" she asked wryly.

"Come on, Lisa, give me credit for a little more backbone than that. Didn't we agree to be friends?"

"Yes," she said softly. Tears stung the backs of Lisa's eyelids. So far, Bruce seemed to be her *only* friend.

"Okay, then how about dinner tomorrow night?" he asked.

"I . . . I may have to work late."

"Let's make it Wednesday night then."

"I'm really not sure," she hedged. "Why don't you call me toward the end of the week?"

Lisa didn't know why she was reluctant to make a date with Bruce. Logan's disapproval had nothing to do with it, she assured herself. It was just that she was too tired tonight to think straight.

Eventually, Bruce gave up trying to wear her down, warning, however, that he intended to keep calling.

Logan was out of the office most of the time during the next couple of days. Without the electric charge of his personality, everything was predictably routine, but there was a strange undercurrent around the studio that bothered Lisa. It wasn't anything she could put her finger on, yet she sensed a difference in the attitude of people around her. While they were all cordial, no one really stopped to talk the way they had before. It was almost as though she was coming down with something they didn't want to catch.

The mystery was solved when she came back from a solitary lunch to find a newspaper on her desk, carefully folded to a Hollywood gossip column. To be sure there was no chance of her missing it, one paragraph was circled in red pencil. Lisa's idle interest turned to consternation as she read:

"Rumor has it that all is not well between that big movie mogul and his secretary (the temporary one). Although he put the Off Limits sign on her around his own studio, the lady found an independent (or should that read rash?) producer who wasn't intimidated. Pretty risky we say. The Big Guy can marshal up a lot of revenge, and he brooks no competition."

The paper fluttered from Lisa's nerveless fingers. The writer hadn't left anything to guesswork, had he? He actually spelled out their names.

The enormity of it hit her as puzzling things suddenly

became clear—like the reason why no one asked her for a date anymore, and the way everyone was being very wary of her now. This was an industry that thrived on gossip. The confrontation between Logan and Bruce on Sunday was probably common knowledge throughout the lot, so everybody was waiting to see if she was in or out of favor before they risked being friendly toward her.

A wave of helpless rage swept over Lisa. The people here were beneath contempt—including the one who had left the paper on her desk—but it was Logan whom her anger was directed against. Had he actually warned everyone not to date her? How dare he? Ever since their paths had crossed he had been trying to direct her life. Well, it was going to stop right now!

Lisa marched next door to Logan's office, throwing open the door without bothering to knock. He was talking on the telephone and he paused, looking up in surprise.

"I want to talk to you," she told him, holding herself stiffly erect.

After cutting his conversation short, he regarded her with raised eyebrows. "Correct me if I'm wrong, but isn't it customary to knock?"

She didn't dignify that with an answer. Waving the newspaper she had brought, Lisa demanded, "Have you read this?"

He took the paper from her negligently. "I don't know, what is it?" His face hardened after he read the first few words, turning to granite by the time he had finished. "Where did you get this?"

"Someone was kind enough to leave it on my desk."

"They should have lined the garbage can with it," he said grimly.

"It's true, isn't it, Logan?"

He got up so swiftly that the casters on the deep leather chair screeched protestingly. "You shouldn't let this trash upset you. Haven't you learned by now what people in this industry are capable of?"

"Including you?" Lisa's emerald eyes sent out sparks of

fire. "How *could* you, Logan? How could you deliberately give the impression that I was your private property?"

His eyes narrowed ominously. "You choose to believe that tripe?"

"How can I help it? You've always warned me against movie people, but I didn't think you would go to these lengths."

He folded his arms, leaning against the desk. "I'm sorry you're so upset at missing out on a few dates, but I can assure you, I never uttered a single word of prohibition."

"You didn't have to! You have other ways of making your displeasure known, and no one on this lot would risk crossing you."

Logan's mouth curved contemptuously. "Those are the kinds of men you feel I cheated you out of?"

"That's not the point," she said hotly.

His eyes were like chips of ice. "I fail to agree with you."

"Then you admit that everything in that article is true," she cried.

Logan rounded the desk, towering over her menacingly. "I don't admit or deny anything. I don't have to justify myself to you."

Lisa flung her head back challengingly. "The great Logan Marshall lives by his own rules, is that it?"

His fingers bit into her shoulders. "I'd like to shake some sense into that empty little head of yours," he grated.

"No one appointed you my guardian," she said furiously. "I'm a grown woman and I'm entitled to make my own mistakes." Pulling out of his grip, she started for the door.

"Where are you going?" he demanded.

She turned with her hand on the knob. "You were right about one thing, I don't like this business. I'm getting out."

"You're leaving me in the lurch?" he asked ominously.

"Oh, Logan, don't be ridiculous! You don't need

me—you never did. I know about Mrs. Livingstone now too. She didn't ask for time off, you made her take it." If Lisa had needed any confirmation, the slight shifting of Logan's gaze provided it. "I guess I have been as stupid as you supposed," she swept on, "but no more. I'm leaving."

"What are you going to do?" he asked.

"That's my problem, not yours," she told him, going out the door.

Lisa cleared her desk out swiftly, half afraid that Logan would come after her. When he didn't, she breathed a sigh of relief, mixed with just a slight twinge of disappointment. Evidently Logan was perfectly willing to see her go. Well, that was just fine with her.

She marched out of the building and down to her parking space, wheeling the trusty Morris out the gate for the last time. The momentum of her anger carried her that far, but practicality soon intruded. What was she going to do now? The confidence with which she had told Logan she could handle her own affairs was seeping away. She had no job, very little money and no friends.

Lisa took a deep breath, steadying herself before the panic that was clogging her throat could stampede her. What was she so worried about? There were other jobs in the world. She had gotten along before Logan entered her life, and she would get along again.

The thought didn't bring the cheer it should have. Underneath her anger and disillusionment was the knowledge that she would never see him again. The realization brought a crushing weight of depression. How could she still care about a man that devious? A man who would do anything to get what he wanted? There was no answer to that. Love knows no reason.

While she was driving around aimlessly, a thought started to take shape. She did have one friend in this town—Bruce. Maybe he would help her get a job. The one thing she had proved at Magnum Studios was that she was a good secretary. Perhaps Bruce, with his wide connections, would know of a secretarial job available. It provided a small ray of hope and she stopped at the first phone booth she saw.

It seemed like an endless amount of time until they located him, causing Lisa to have second thoughts. Was she presuming on a very short friendship? People in this business were very cynical about being asked for favors. Their refusals weren't always kind. Her hands were clammy and she was on the point of hanging up when Bruce's voice sounded in her ear.

"Lisa, darling, this is an unexpected surprise."

His genuine warmth brought tears to her eyes. "Oh, Bruce," was all she could manage.

"What's the matter, honey?"

"It's . . . nothing is the matter," she said shakily.

"You sound like you're crying."

"No, I . . . I'm fine."

"You don't sound like it. Are you at the studio?"

"No, I'm in a phone booth someplace," she told him.

"What do you mean someplace? Tell me where you are and I'll come and get you." His voice was filled with concern.

"That isn't necessary. I'm all right, really I am."

"I'll believe that when I see you. If you won't let me come there, then you come here." He gave her his address. "We're shooting in Studio B. Just give your name to the guard and he'll let you in."

"Oh, Bruce, I'm sorry. I didn't realize you were in production. I shouldn't have disturbed you at work."

"Don't be a little idiot," he said impatiently. "I'll expect you shortly."

"Wait! Don't hang up," Lisa cried. "There is something I'd better tell you first in case it changes anything. I quit my job with Logan."

"Good! You can come to work for me," Bruce said decisively. "Why would you think it would make any difference to me?"

"Well, I'm not exactly the people's choice at Magnum. I thought maybe . . ."

"Lisa, you little nut." He chuckled affectionately. "Get your delectable self over here as fast as possible."

She hung up the receiver slowly, a sense of relief making her legs feel wobbly.

It took quite a while to get to the vast facilities where he was shooting. Then it took what seemed like another age to find the correct studio. The huge television city was a rabbit warren of rehearsal rooms, offices and sound stages. In addition, guided tours for out-of-towners were being conducted. Lisa was bitterly amused when she saw people whispering behind their hands, wondering if she were "somebody." *I'm not anybody,* she wanted to tell them, *not even the great Logan Marshall's secretary anymore.*

"What took you so long, honey?" Bruce asked when Lisa eventually managed to find her way to Studio B. "I was getting worried."

The large sound stage was being set up for another scene, the huge klieg lights temporarily darkened. Bruce left the group of people surrounding him, coming over to Lisa with a clipboard in his hand holding pages of script.

"You're busy," she said apologetically. "I shouldn't be here."

"Nonsense, I'm never too busy for you. Besides, I want to know what the devil is going on."

"I called because I . . . I wanted to talk to you about something, but it can wait until you're through."

He took her arm, steering her into a small office. "Whatever has you this upset is something I want to know about now. It involves Logan, doesn't it?"

She looked down at her clasped hands. "I told you I quit my job."

"Why?" he asked bluntly. "What did he do to you?"

"He didn't . . . it wasn't . . ." Lisa took a deep breath. "Did you read the *Courier* today? The 'Hollywood Hot Line' column?"

Bruce shook his head. "Haven't had time." He looked over the cluttered desk. "It should be here someplace." After locating the paper, he turned rapidly to the entertainment section, scanning the column she had mentioned. "I see," he said slowly.

"So will everyone else," she cried. "But it isn't true!"

"What difference does it make?" Bruce shrugged. "You knew what people were saying."

She sprang to her feet, pacing nervously. "Gossip is one thing, but seeing it in print like this will make everybody believe it."

"What did Logan say?"

"He was angry. He said pretty much what you said. He also said he hadn't warned anyone to stay away from me."

"There is more than one way to build a fence," Bruce said dryly. It was what Lisa had accused Logan of and she looked away. Bruce continued to regard her steadily. "I've known Logan long enough to know that his behavior toward you is uncharacteristic, to say the least. Oh, he's possessive enough. He never wants anyone to get in his way until he's through with a woman. But competition never made him this paranoid. Still, if you say there is nothing between you two, I'll believe you, Lisa—even though it's a little difficult."

Her shoulders sagged. "What you're really saying is that you *don't* believe me."

"No, I just think there is more here than meets the eye. How do you feel about him?" Bruce asked abruptly.

Lisa glanced over his shoulder. "I . . . he's been very kind to me. He helped me when I was very sick once," she said without elaborating.

"That's all it is, just gratitude?" he persisted.

"Of course." She forced herself to meet his searching gaze. "That also explains Logan's solicitude where I'm concerned. We became very friendly when I was convalescing and he regards me as sort of a . . . a kid sister."

Bruce's skepticism showed; however, he decided not to

pursue the subject. "Well, it's over and done with in any case. What are you going to do now?"

"That's what I wanted to talk to you about. I thought you might know of someone who is looking for a secretary." She waited anxiously for his answer. When it came, it wasn't what she was hoping for.

"You're wasted behind a typewriter, honey. How would you like to be an actress?"

"Oh, Bruce, you know I don't have any talent."

"That has never been determined. Why don't you let me be the judge?"

"I wouldn't have the first idea of what to do," she said helplessly.

"You don't have to, I'll lead you by the hand. We're starting a new TV show next week and there is a part in it that's made to order for you. It's just a small part, but it will be a way of getting your feet wet." He rummaged around the cluttered desk. "There's a working script here somewhere. Ah, here it is. You'll play the part of Carrie. Take it home and learn the lines. Tomorrow I'll expect you to read for me."

Lisa clutched the bulky script he had thrust into her arms. "I can't let you do this for me, Bruce. I could be the biggest bomb since they split the atom."

"You could also turn out to be a very big star. I'm not doing it for you, I'm doing it for myself. You're going to make me famous."

His transparent kindness brought tears to her eyes. "You don't need me for that. I appreciate your generosity, but—"

"I forgot to mention the salary," he interrupted, naming a figure that made her gasp. "Does that change your mind?"

Lisa had been determined to turn down what she was sure was an act of charity. The amount of money made her pause. The low state of her cash reserve was worrying in light of the fact that the rent and utility bills would be due soon. This was only a temporary solution, but since the alternative was going back to sales work, Lisa decided to take it. After all, why not? He said it was only a small part; probably nobody would notice whether she was good or bad.

"If you're really sure I won't cause you any embarrassment," she said slowly.

"It's going to be a pleasure having you around," Bruce assured her. Putting his arm around her shoulders, he walked her to the door. "Now I really have to get back to work. I'll see you first thing tomorrow morning, honey."

Chapter Eight

The first day on the set, Lisa was terrified. It had been bad enough auditioning for Bruce, but at least he was a friend. She credited his enthusiasm to that, refusing to believe him when he said she had a natural talent.

"I mean it, Lisa. Of course there are all kinds of stage business bits you have to learn, but that's purely mechanical. The important thing is that you have a rare kind of believability."

The director agreed with him, while the cameraman was entranced with the perfect contours of her face and figure. It was a different cameraman than Rudy Mandell, for which Lisa was grateful. She hadn't liked him.

The only cloud on the horizon was Belva Crystal, the star of the show they were filming. She was a mature actress on the verge of being phased into character parts. Her tightly girdled figure, which had once been voluptuous, was now frankly plump. Nor could her carefully raised head hide the incipient double chin. Still, she was a big name, possessing undoubted talent. The problem was that she refused to age gracefully and had an almost paranoid suspicion of younger actresses, being sure they were all out to steal scenes from her.

Lisa longed to reassure Belva that she had nothing to

fear from her, knowing all the while that it was useless. It would only be insulting to tell someone that you wanted no part of her job, regarding her life's work as being rather childish. She solved the problem by staying out of Belva's way as much as possible.

The part of Carrie was small, as Bruce had promised. Lisa played the role of the star's younger sister. Except for Belva's criticism and occasional outbursts, Lisa found the job easy enough. Everyone on the set was friendly, and of course Bruce was tremendously supportive.

Their friendship was something she came to depend on. Besides seeing each other every day on the set, they had frequent dates. It was true that he sometimes tried to make love to her, but when she indicated that he was out of line, Bruce never pursued it.

Lisa constantly reminded herself of how lucky she was, ignoring the emptiness that filled her. She refused to think of the past, building protective layers around her heart that were ripped to shreds by one phone call from Logan.

"Lisa?" The remembered deep voice did funny things to her pulse. "How are you getting along?"

"Just . . . just fine," she quavered. "How are you, Logan?"

"I'm surprised you remembered my name," he said dryly.

"Don't be silly. You would be hard to forget." That was more true than he knew.

"You too, Lisa." His voice softened for a moment, then became curt again. "What are you doing with yourself? Are you working?"

"Yes." She contented herself with the one word.

"Back at the department store?" he asked grimly.

"No," she murmured, knowing that Logan wouldn't let it go at that. She was right.

"Where then?"

She considered refusing to answer, giving it up almost immediately. Logan could always get anything out of her, and wouldn't hesitate to do so. With a sense of fatality, she said, "I'm working for Bruce."

"Doing what?" The two words were encased in ice.

"I'm . . . I'm working on a television show of his."

"I have all night, Lisa. If it takes that long, so be it. But understand this—I intend to find out what you're doing," Logan said implacably.

"All right, I'm acting!" she cried. "I didn't want to tell you because I know how you feel about it, but it beats selling dresses at Bullock's."

There was a short silence. Then, "Congratulations, Lisa. You really had me fooled." The contempt in his voice made her flinch. "You were after an acting career all along, weren't you? Too bad you didn't hang on here a little longer, though. If you had played your cards right, I might have sponsored you myself."

His withering scorn desolated Lisa. It would be useless to try to tell him that she had taken the job purely for economic reasons. Logan was convinced that she was just a cheap opportunist. His anger fairly crackled across the line. Before he could loose a flood of searing recriminations which Lisa knew she couldn't endure, she quietly hung up the phone.

The next day her eyes were heavy from lack of sleep. Hank Pulver, the cameraman, remarked disapprovingly, "You got to cut out the partying till we get a wrap, sweetheart. Those shadows under your eyes don't make my work any easier."

Bruce noticed them too. "Is anything wrong, honey?" he asked.

"Just an attack of nerves I suppose." Lisa smiled wanly. "I guess it just occurred to me how many people are going to see this show we're filming."

Bruce put his arms around her waist, lifting her off the floor and twirling her around. "This is just the beginning, baby. Today a bit part, tomorrow the world."

He was so exuberant that she couldn't tell him it wasn't what she wanted. Logan was right, making films wasn't that much fun. Lisa didn't know which was worse, the boredom or Belva's tantrums. Fortunately, television shows didn't take too long. In a very short time they would be finished, then she could look for a real job. The large salary that had seduced her into this had proved to be a mirage. By the time she joined the union, a necessity in the industry, and paid various dues, there was very little left.

The day of the wrap, as the finish of the show was called, Bruce told her about a party being held that night.

"It's at Will Westbury's home, the big banker. Wait till you see his estate, it's a real stunner."

She shook her head. "I don't want to go, Bruce."

"Are you kidding? Everybody in the industry will be there."

"I'm not really part of the industry."

"Of course you are. You're a card-carrying actress."

"With the shortest career in history." She smiled. "We both know that this part was just a fluke."

"There will be other parts, honey. I don't have anything for you at the moment, but I'll make a few calls and we'll find you another job. Maybe we can even make some contacts at the party tonight. That's the way it's done more often than not."

"You don't understand, Bruce. I'm very grateful to you for tiding me over a bad time, but I'm okay now. I'm going to look for a secretarial job."

"You honestly mean it, don't you?" He stared at her incredulously. "You don't give a damn about a career, do you?"

"Not as an actress. It was fun and I'm glad I did it, but it's time to go back to the real world."

"You are truly one of a kind, Lisa." His hand stroked her gleaming hair gently. "All right, have it your own way, but at least come to the party with me tonight. You wouldn't deprive me of the joy of showing off the most beautiful girl in town, would you?"

Lisa honestly didn't want to go, yet it was little enough to do for Bruce, so she agreed.

She dressed carefully that night, wanting to be a credit to him. Unfortunately, the only evening gown she had was the green chiffon she had worn at that fateful dinner at Logan's. It brought back memories so painful that Lisa didn't think she could bear them. That was silly, she told herself firmly. It was time she forgot her schoolgirl infatuation and got on with her life. Wearing the dress again would be the first step. After all, it was only a length of material; it didn't have any power for good or evil. When she stepped into it, however, Lisa had an unpleasant premonition.

It wasn't in evidence when Bruce picked her up. Her shining auburn hair was pulled up and back, trailing masses of waves and ringlets down her slender neck. Artful makeup made her eyes look like faceted emeralds, matching the color of the seductive gown that clung lovingly to her body. Her skin had the creamy glow of a cultured pearl, and her lips were touched with a gloss that highlighted her full, sensitive mouth.

Bruce's reaction was a low wolf whistle as he inspected her lingeringly. "I said I was bringing the most beautiful girl in this town—I should have made that the world!"

She whirled around for his inspection. "I'm glad you like it, it's the only gown I have."

His hands fastened around her slim waist, drawing her very close. "I'd like you equally well without it," he murmured.

"We'd better get going," Lisa said nervously. "It will take forever to get to Bel-Air in the traffic."

Bruce held her a moment longer before releasing her. "Whatever you say, doll."

The party was held in a mansion that was everything he

had promised. A curving driveway cut through manicured lawns to a large pink house with ornamental grillwork in the style of a New Orleans plantation manor. Lights were blazing from every window, and music from several different orchestras floated out and mingled on the night air.

White-coated parking attendants whisked the cars away, and a black-clad butler stood at the front door. A maid in a frilly white apron stood at his side, her sole duty to relieve the female guests of their coats.

A broad entry hall led through to the patio at the back of the house. Beyond it, a huge swimming pool shaped like a four-leaf clover was lit with underwater lights. Gardenias bobbed around on the surface of the water, while two girls in sequined bathing suits swam languidly back and forth. Presumably they were part of the entertainment, although none of the guests seemed to be paying any attention.

The ones who weren't gathered around the buffet tables, laden with enough food to do justice to Henry VIII's court, were clustered around the numerous bars or dancing under a huge red and white tent that had been erected, along with a portable dance floor, on the spacious lawn.

"I feel like I just stepped into a nineteen-fifties musical," Lisa murmured.

"Will would be delighted. That was his era, and he can't believe the parade has gone by," Bruce said dryly.

As though answering to his name, a tall, distinguished, silver-haired man joined them. "Bruce, how nice to see you." He held out his hand without taking his eyes off Lisa. "And who is this charming young lady?"

"Lisa Brooks, may I present Wilroy P. Westbury," Bruce said.

"Why the formality?" the older man asked disapprovingly. "Call me Will," he said, taking Lisa's hand. "All my friends do and I hope to count you as one of them."

"That's very kind of you, Mr. . . . uh . . . Will."

"You're new in town, aren't you, my dear?"

"Fairly so. I've been here almost four months." It didn't

seem possible to Lisa that so much could have happened in such a short time.

"What do you think of our city?" the banker asked.

"It's lovely. And so is your home," she said, looking at the graceful balconies that ornamented the upper floor of the spacious mansion.

"Would you like me to show you around?" Will asked.

Bruce entered the conversation. "I think Lisa needs a drink first. She has a terribly parched look." When her eyes flew to his face in surprised denial, he took her arm firmly. "Come along to the bar, darling. We'll see you later, Will."

"Why did you do that?" she asked, as Bruce led her away. "I would like to have seen the house."

"Your tour would have consisted of one room—his bedroom," Bruce informed her cynically.

"That's ridiculous! That nice old man?"

"Better not let him hear you call him that. Even with the 'nice' in front of it," he chuckled.

"You're teasing me, aren't you, Bruce?" At the look on his face, she said incredulously, "But I just met him."

"At Will's age you don't have much time." He shrugged. "He's a lecherous old goat, but he can do a lot for a girl if he likes her."

"That's disgusting!"

"I thought you'd feel that way." He laughed, putting his arm around her shoulders. "Have a drink and relax, honey."

Their progress to the bar was slow, since Bruce was greeted repeatedly. Lisa met so many people that she couldn't remember their names, except for the ones recognizable as personalities on television or in the movies. It was indeed a glittering assemblage.

The conversation was mainly shoptalk, and although Bruce was careful to include her, Lisa felt herself to be an encumbrance. After a while, she edged away, murmuring something about going to the powder room. The bartender was supplying a fresh drink to Bruce, who smiled vaguely and told her to hurry back. As soon as she left, he was involved in animated conversation again.

Lisa drifted aimlessly toward the house, not knowing quite what to do with herself. Maybe she would go and fix her makeup after all. As she got to the patio, a man blocked her path.

"Well, hello. I haven't seen you before," he told Lisa, looking her up and down with X-ray eyes.

It was Craig Bohrman, an actor who played the detective in a popular weekly series. He was quite handsome, although Lisa was surprised to note that he was much shorter than he appeared on television.

"Who do you belong to?" he asked.

"I don't belong to anyone," she said coldly.

Her displeasure was wasted on him. "Oh, a free agent, huh? That's good. You're a pretty little thing. Let's find a quiet corner where we can get acquainted and discuss your future."

"No, thank you," she snapped.

"Aw, come on, baby. Loosen up and be friendly." His hand fastened around her wrist.

Lisa struggled to free herself. "Would you kindly let go of me?"

A deep voice with a hint of menace interrupted them. "The lady isn't one of your fans, Craig. I suggest you buzz off."

Lisa looked up into Logan's cold blue eyes as the actor gave an embarrassed laugh and released her.

"Sure, Logan, I . . . uh . . . we were just kidding around."

Craig faded hurriedly into the crowd, leaving Lisa to stare wordlessly up at Logan. He looked so handsome in the stark black and white of his evening clothes. After never expecting to see him again, Lisa hadn't had time to prepare herself for it. His sheer physical impact was so devastating that she felt her legs start to tremble.

Logan's hard eyes swept over her, taking in every detail

of the clinging green chiffon, and Lisa wondered if he was remembering the last time she had worn the dress.

"Should I apologize for chasing off your latest conquest?" he asked. "Perhaps my intrusion was unwarranted."

"Oh, no, I'm very grateful," she said breathlessly. "He . . . he was rather unpleasant."

"But fairly typical of what you'll meet here tonight. Congratulations, by the way. You hit the big time fast. An invitation to one of Westbury's parties isn't easy to come by, appearances to the contrary," Logan said, looking out over the hordes of expensively dressed people.

"I don't suppose I was actually invited." At Logan's raised eyebrows, Lisa added reluctantly, "I'm here with Bruce."

Logan's face hardened, yet his voice remained casual. "It doesn't matter, you would be welcome with or without a date. Will dotes on beautiful women. Wait until he sees you."

"He already has," Lisa said shortly.

Logan gave a bark of humorless laughter. "You do get around, don't you? I can see that my chivalrous intervention a minute ago was quite unnecessary."

"That's not true," she protested. "I was very happy that you got rid of that ham actor."

"Even though people might misconstrue it?" he asked mockingly. "They might think you were my—what did you call it?—private property."

Lisa sighed. "I was angry, Logan, can't you understand that?"

"Were you, Lisa? Or was it just a good excuse?" he asked softly.

"I don't know what you mean."

"I think you do. I believe that under that beautiful, scheming face of yours lies a crumb of conscience. When Bruce offered you what you really wanted, a chance at an acting career, you didn't know how to tell me. So you provoked an argument to give you a convenient excuse for leaving."

She looked at him in outrage. "I suppose I planted that article in the *Courier* too?"

Logan shrugged. "Just a fortuitous accident. If it hadn't been that, you would have found another pretext."

"You can't honestly believe that," she whispered.

His eyes were appraising as they lingered on the curve of her cheek before moving to the wide, tremulous mouth. "Who am I to sit in judgment? With the face of an angel and the body of Circe, why shouldn't you parlay them into fame and fortune?"

"I never wanted to be an actress," she cried. "I still don't. It was just a way of—" she stopped as his strong hand closed around her throat, the long fingers digging momentarily into the side of her neck before relaxing in a caressing manner.

"I suppose I should be flattered that you care enough about my good opinion to lie, but it isn't necessary, Lisa. The only thing I regret is that you weren't honest with me in the beginning. I could have done as much for you as Bruce—with no strings attached. Or was that the problem?" A long forefinger traced the low neckline of her gown. "Was it my failure to take you up on your kind offer the first time that drove you into Bruce's arms?"

Lisa flushed, her long eyelashes veiling the misery in her emerald eyes. "Logan, don't!"

He forced her chin up. "Did Bruce solve the compelling mystery for you, or was that all a lie too?" he asked harshly.

She jerked her chin away, running blindly toward the house. In the mirrored powder room that threw back countless fragmented reflections, Lisa locked the door, leaning against it until her pounding heart slowed its beat.

How could Logan believe such vile things about her? His wounding words echoed in her brain, shocking her with their savagery. Even during their most bitter arguments, he had never spoken to her like that. It was like a nightmare, but what was reality? Had she just imagined the gentle lover who had held her in his arms, caressing her so lovingly that her awakened passion had almost exceeded his?

Lisa closed her eyes in pain. She must try to forget those tender moments. Logan was lost to her for all time. Whatever small measure of affection he had once felt for her was gone forever.

Lisa couldn't even summon anger at his unjust accusations. She was too crushed by the inexplicable things that had happened to her.

After a great while, she forced herself to rejoin the party. Lisa didn't realize how long she had been gone until she found Bruce at a different bar, and noticed the flush on his cheekbones. He had evidently had quite a few drinks.

His voice was steady though, as he greeted her. "I was about to send out a search party, honey. Willy didn't corner you, did he?"

"No, I . . . I was just talking to some people."

"Good," he said approvingly. "Are you having a good time?"

"Yes, lovely," she answered brightly.

More people joined them and Lisa made an effort to join in the conversation. When someone asked her to dance she accepted, going through the motions while smiling mechanically. Someone else escorted her to the buffet table where she filled a plate that she barely touched. Lisa couldn't complain about being neglected, although Bruce rarely strayed far from one bar or another.

He was always surrounded by a group, mostly of men, and he always had a drink in his hand. He looked for her frequently, beckoning her to join him, but Lisa found it difficult to become interested in the conversation. Especially since she was conscious of Logan watching her from a distance, a sardonic smile playing over his mobile mouth.

After what seemed like weeks, Lisa couldn't take any more. There was no question of asking Bruce if he was ready to leave; he looked like he was set for the night.

What she needed was a breather, Lisa decided, a few moments completely alone.

Beyond the lighted party area, the estate stretched on for acres. Flagstone paths lined with carefully tended beds of flowers wound through the lawn in graceful curves ending in a thick stand of tall trees. White wrought-iron benches gleamed in the deep shadows, drawing Lisa irresistibly in that direction.

It was chilly and she shivered in her gossamer dress, but the peace and quiet more than made up for the slight discomfort. After a while she sank down on one of the benches. It was so restful, with the music muted to a pleasant level at this distance, that she leaned her head back and closed her eyes. The thick grass muffled approaching footsteps, and Lisa gave a frightened yelp when a hand stroked her cheek.

"What are you doing out here all alone?" Bruce asked.

"You startled me," she gasped.

"I didn't mean to," he apologized. "I got worried about you. I missed you."

"I didn't think you would notice. You were surrounded by a mob when I left."

"I'm sorry, Lisa, I didn't mean to neglect you."

"You didn't," she said quickly. "I've been amusing myself."

"These big bashes are all alike," he said ruefully. "Everyone wants to bend your ear and if you slight anybody, it gets blown up into an instant feud."

"I understand, Bruce, I wasn't complaining. People have been very nice to me."

"Other men you mean. Don't think I didn't see them trying to make time with my girl."

"I'm not your girl," Lisa said gently.

He sat down on the bench next to her, taking one of her hands and kissing the palm. "I'd like you to be, you know that, don't you?"

The gesture, although innocent enough, was vaguely disturbing. "Bruce, I thought we agreed—"

"I know. We agreed to be friends. It was a great idea except that it won't work. We have to talk, Lisa, and this is as good a time and place as any."

"At a party?" she asked.

"Why not? No one is likely to bother us out here."

The truth of it made her a little nervous. "Nevertheless, it's not good manners," she pointed out, starting to rise.

He caught her wrist, pulling her down beside him. "I couldn't care less about that. I've played the Hollywood game all evening, now I want to be alone with my girl."

"I told you, Bruce—"

"And I'm telling you the way I want it to be," he broke in roughly. "I find that friendship isn't enough, Lisa. I'm a normal male and I can't be with you without wanting to make love to you."

Lisa sighed. "Then I guess we'll have to stop seeing each other."

"You don't mean that." His hand slid under her long hair, pulling her head forward. "We have something good going for us. Why won't you admit it and just let it happen?"

His mouth closed over hers, forcing it to open to the invasion of his tongue. She could taste the Scotch he had consumed and her nose wrinkled with distaste. When she tried to push him away his arms tightened painfully, arousing the first twinges of fear. She started to struggle in earnest now, finally succeeding in breaking his hold.

"You're drunk," she accused coldly.

He shook his head. "It would take a lot more than I've had. I'll admit my inhibitions have broken down some, but I'm only saying what I would have gotten around to sooner or later. I want you, Lisa, and if you'll just relax with me, I can make you want me too."

"It's no good, Bruce. I told you when we met how it would have to be."

His mouth touched the hollow in her throat while his hands slid up her ribs. "I intend to change your mind."

His questing hands sent ripples of revulsion shuddering

through her. Pushing hard against his chest, she cried, "Let go of me, Bruce."

He gripped her wrists, pulling her arms behind her back and securing them there with one hand while his other continued to caress her. His body half covered hers as he forced her back along the bench, his breathing harsh.

"You don't understand, Lisa. I'm not talking about a one night stand, I'm talking about a permanent arrangement. I want you to move in with me."

"You must be out of your mind!" she cried.

"Sometimes I think I am." He was raining fevered kisses on her face and neck, his avid mouth descending to the valley between her breasts. "You don't know what it's been like these past weeks, being with you every day and not being able to touch you. I've never felt this way about a woman before."

"That's because you have never had a relationship that didn't include sex," she said scornfully.

His hands gripped her face hard. "No, that's *not* it! I'm falling in love with you, don't you understand? I'll even marry you if that's what you want."

"If it's the only way you can get me, you mean," she said tightly. "Well, you can put your mind at ease. I don't want to marry you—and I'm not going to let you make love to me either."

"Aren't you?" he asked softly.

Lisa felt a flash of terror as she looked up at his passion-swollen face. His arousal was all too evident when he covered her shrinking body with his, rendering her helpless by his weight. She struggled frantically in a battle he was bound to win, knowing it was useless, just as pleading with him would be.

Lisa cringed away from the hateful mouth that roamed across her face. A thin scream of terror was wrenched from her. This couldn't be happening with people so close—and yet so far away.

She was almost exhausted by her struggles when, suddenly, Bruce's crushing weight was abruptly lifted from her. Lisa looked up to see Logan's furious face glaring down at her. As though in a trance, she watched as he aimed a murderous right to Bruce's jaw. Bruce went down almost in slow motion, but Logan wasn't satisfied. His eyes were demonic as he grabbed a handful of the inert man's shirt and started to drag him to his feet, his fist cocked once more.

That galvanized Lisa. "No, Logan, you'll kill him!"

"That's what I aim to do," he grated between clenched teeth.

She sprang to her feet, clutching at his arm, unaware of her tear-stained face. At least it distracted him from Bruce.

"What did he do to you?" he demanded grimly.

"Nothing. You came along before he—" her voice broke. "Oh, Logan!" She buried her face against his chest, the tears coming in a flood.

Logan's comforting arms closed around her. He stroked her hair, making soothing sounds while the wrenching sobs racked her body. When she was finally quiet, he took off his jacket and put it around her.

"Come on, I'm taking you home," he said tightly.

He didn't utter a single word in the car, discouraging Lisa from doing so by the hard profile he turned to her. In the dim light from the dashboard, Logan's face looked like it was carved out of granite. All the tenderness he had briefly shown was gone now. When they reached her house, the fingers that gripped her arm were like steel.

Inside her apartment, Lisa turned toward Logan. Bitter humor curled his mouth. She drew a quick breath, averting her eyes from his as she turned wordlessly toward the bedroom. Logan's hand jerked her back.

"What provoked that attack of Bruce's tonight? Were you trying to walk out on him too?" he asked, his eyes hard. "Did you make better connections at the party? Like Westbury for instance?"

The contempt in his voice flicked her like a whip. "How can you say that?" she whispered.

"I thought I put it very delicately," he mocked. "I could have asked if you had to give Will a sample first."

Lisa started to tremble. "You're detestable!"

"I don't think I'd start calling names. There are a few rather unpleasant ones that could be applied to you."

Logan's brutal treatment, on top of all she had been through that night, snapped Lisa's control. She stood up to him with eyes like blazing emeralds in her white face. "All right, you guessed it, I was walking out on Bruce because Mr. Westbury made me a better offer. I admit it. Is that what you want to hear?"

His long fingers fastened around her neck, biting into the soft flesh while he stared at her with untamed fury. "If I thought that—"

"Why does it shock you?" she broke in recklessly. "Isn't that how girls get ahead in this town? Why should I be any different?" She gave a high, unnatural laugh. "Actually, I have you to thank. I might not have thought of it if you hadn't given me the idea."

"Stop it!" He shook her so savagely that her fine, silky hair flew into disarray. "I don't believe you!"

She was wild with self-destruction. "Why should you doubt it? Didn't I throw myself at *you?* Fortunately, other men were more receptive."

His already agonizing grip tightened. "You're lying!" he snarled.

Suddenly, the fight went out of Lisa, leaving her drained and uncaring. "Of course I'm lying, but you won't believe that either." Tears welled up in her eyes, trickling down her pale cheeks.

The fury left Logan as he gently touched her wet cheek, his face tortured. "Lisa, I'm sorry. I—"

She turned away, his jacket slipping from her shoulders. "Just go, Logan," she said wearily.

His arms went around her waist, pulling her back against him. "You need me, Lisa. Don't you know that yet?" She shook her head, trying to break away, but he tightened his hold, burying his face in her scented hair. "I told you how it was out there, you wouldn't believe me. Come back, Lisa. Let me take care of you."

His hands slid caressingly over her midriff, moving up to touch her breasts. The sensation caused a shudder of desire even though she willed her treacherous body not to react. It was no use. Logan could tell. She had to make an effort, though.

"Let me go, Logan," she pleaded in a low voice.

His teeth gently worked the soft skin of her earlobe while his fingertips lightly skimmed her breasts, pausing at the hardened peaks. "Are you sure that's what you want?"

"Yes," she said, gasping as she tried to capture his tormenting hands.

"Look at me and tell me that." Turning her gently in his arms, his lips brushed hers in a feathery caress that was tantalizing. He smiled down into her dazzled eyes. "Say it now, Lisa."

She couldn't. He was so close that their breath mingled, yet it wasn't close enough. His provocative mouth was driving her to distraction. Lisa felt that if Logan didn't kiss her soon she would surely lose control and beg him to.

As though recognizing her need, Logan's head bent slowly to hers, his lips teasing hers apart with a practiced sensuality that fanned the flames of desire already consuming her.

Lisa's trembling body was molded to his hard lines, further seducing her will to resist. She gloried in the feel of his muscular thighs digging into hers, and she touched the strong column of his neck with tentative little caresses. It had been so long and she wanted him so much, wanted his mouth to continue its fiery exploration of her throat and shoulders, wanted his hands to explore every part of her eager body.

With a sigh of surrender, she relaxed against him, twining her slim fingers in his thick dark hair. When he lifted her in his arms and carried her into the bedroom, she clung tightly to him, refusing to think beyond this moment.

He put her gently on the bed, lying beside her and cradling her tenderly. A low chuckle of triumph sounded in his throat as her arms stole around his neck.

"You're mine, Lisa. You know it now, don't you?" His drugging kiss didn't allow her to answer. "You'll never get away from me again," he muttered thickly. "This is what I should have done in the very beginning."

Her eyes fluttered open, flinching at the naked victory she saw in his. Despair chilled Lisa's blood at the look on Logan's face. There was exultation, there was conquest and jubilation—there was everything except love. What a fool she was! Logan wanted her certainly, but passion wasn't the main consideration. She represented winning and losing to him. She was the nagging one who had gotten away, the one who had spoiled his perfect record. Lisa had known he didn't love her, yet for the most intimate act between a man and a woman, there should at least be affection, *some* measure of caring.

Turning her head aside to hide the pain, she tried to draw away, resisting when Logan pulled her back. "What is it, darling?" he asked.

"Let me go, Logan. I can't do it."

"Don't be frightened, sweetheart," he murmured soothingly.

She shook her head. "It isn't that. I just don't want you to make love to me."

His hand swung her chin around sharply. "You're lying! Would you like me to prove it?"

"No!" Long eyelashes shaded her downcast eyes. "All right, I do want you. You're very experienced and you know how to make that happen, but it doesn't change things."

"In the name of God, *why?*"

"Because I don't want you to own me body and soul." Lisa was horrified as the revealing words slipped out, but Logan was too angry to realize their import.

"You're not going to do it to me again, Lisa," he said tautly. "This time you've gone too far to stop. I'm going to take you, and nothing in heaven or hell is going to stop me."

His hard mouth claimed hers in a punishing, bruising kiss which Lisa passively endured. When he lifted his head to glare at her, she looked back at him steadily.

"You're not really any different than Bruce, are you?" she asked quietly.

There was a long pause while Logan stared at her, warring emotions playing over his face. Then, with a muttered oath, he got up and strode out the door.

Lisa watched him go, feeling as though all the life were draining out of her. Turning facedown on the bed, she wondered how long it would take her to die.

Chapter Nine

The telephone rang several times that night, but Lisa ignored it. Whether it was Logan or Bruce made no difference. She didn't want to talk to either of them.

In the morning the doorbell rang and she ignored that too. When the phone started again, Lisa knew she had to get out of the house. Dressing quickly, she started out the front door, almost tripping over a long, white florist's box.

Inside were a dozen white and a dozen red roses. The card read:

> "I couldn't remember which color is
> for forgiveness so I'm sending both.
> I love you,
> Bruce."

Lisa put the lovely blooms in water, tossing the card aside carelessly. Nothing seemed to penetrate the coating of ice around her heart. Catching up a sweater, she ran out the door as the phone began to ring again.

The decision to move crystallized in Lisa's mind while she was wandering aimlessly. Bruce had made it obvious that he wasn't going to leave her alone, and who knew what Logan's plans were? Their last encounter was so shattering that he might seek revenge. If that were so, Lisa knew she couldn't stand the form it would take.

After buying a newspaper she went into a small restaurant, marking off some likely prospects over a cup of black coffee. She also looked through the help wanted ads.

It didn't seem possible that such an upheaval could be accomplished in that little time, but a short week later found Lisa ensconced in a new life. Fortunately her apartment had been a furnished one, so moving didn't pose any problem. Finding the job at Mason's department store so fast was another stroke of luck, Lisa supposed. Still, a sense of unreality enveloped her. In a way, she was back to square one—the past few months might never have existed. She had cut all ties, disconnecting her phone and leaving no forwarding address.

The job behind the perfume counter paid enough to live on, with a small amount left over each week to add to her secret fund. Now more than ever, Lisa longed to pay Logan back the money he had spent on her. Although he had undoubtedly written it off as a bad debt, Lisa felt a compulsion to clear the slate. It wouldn't change Logan's opinion of her, but it was necessary for her own self-respect.

If only it wasn't such slow going. Lisa wouldn't demean herself by sending five or ten dollars at a time, an amount that would only advertise her straitened circumstances. She was waiting till she could accumulate a decent sum, something that wasn't easy with the cost of bare necessities these days. Not that she minded denying herself luxuries. There was nothing she wanted to buy. It was a source of perplexity to the other saleswomen.

Lisa knew they were curious about her. It was evidenced by the devious ways in which they tried to dig out details of her private life, finally giving up when she was polite, yet totally uncommunicative. Lisa was living in a protective cocoon, going to work and coming home, fixing a meal which she barely ate, looking listlessly through the newspaper.

One day her anonymity was threatened in an alarming way. Shirley Blassick, one of the other saleswomen, cornered her the first thing in the morning. "Did you by any chance see that television play last night, *A Cup of Kindness?*"

"No, I don't watch television much," Lisa said.

"You should have seen this show, it was great. Belva Crystal starred and there was some girl in it who was the spitting image of you."

"Oh, really?" Lisa murmured, her heart starting to pound.

"I didn't get her name because I guess the credits came on in the beginning while I was finishing the dishes," Shirley said. "Whoever she is, though, she sure looks like you."

Lisa was grateful that a customer appeared just then.

Since she studiously avoided the television column in the paper, indeed the whole entertainment page, Lisa wasn't aware that she had caused a minor sensation. Although hers had been a small part, the production was high budgeted, meriting reviews from the major critics. They were unanimous in their favorable comments on Lisa's talent, adding that they would like to see more of her exquisite face. In Hollywood, that was all that was needed to make a career take off.

Lisa was also unaware of the fact that she was being actively sought. When it became known that she had dropped out of the scene completely, producers became intrigued, redoubling their efforts to find her. One enterprising entrepreneur sent a picture of her to the evening newspaper which printed it under the caption, "Do you know where to find this girl?"

It wasn't long after that a short, balding, paunchy man came up to her counter. "So this is where you've been hiding," he said jovially.

"I beg your pardon?" Lisa looked at him coolly.

"Don't you know everybody in town has been looking for you?"

"I'm afraid you've made a mistake," she said.

"No mistake, honey. You're Lisa Brooks, aren't you?"

A chill of apprehension smote her. "Yes, but I—"

"You led us all a merry chase." He looked at her shrewdly. "Pretty clever move, kid. Did you think it up yourself or have you got a press agent?"

"I don't know what you're talking about, Mr.—"

"Sol Palinski," he told her. "I'm here to offer you a movie contract."

She looked at him with distaste. "Is this a joke, Mr. Palinski?"

"Call me Sol, and it's no joke. I want you to play the lead in a new movie I'm casting. How does that grab you, sweetheart?"

"It doesn't," she told him shortly. "I don't know how you found me, but I wish you hadn't. I'm not interested in a movie career."

"I haven't even mentioned money and already you're bargaining?" he asked aggrievedly.

Her lip curled contemptuously as she realized that he thought she was playing hard to get in order to force the price up. It was typical movie mentality. "Whether you believe it or not, there isn't anything that would make me go back into the entertainment industry. What do you know about me anyway? How do you even know I can act?"

"Are you kidding? Those reviews you got for *A Cup of Kindness* weren't chopped liver. You'll be a smash at the box office."

She looked at him in bewilderment. "But I only had a small part. Do you mean someone actually noticed me?"

"You don't have to put on an act for me, girlie. I'm prepared to make a generous offer." His eyes narrowed appraisingly. "Or has someone gotten to you first? Is that it?"

Lisa felt as though she were trying to make herself understood in a foreign language. This pudgy little man represented everything she had wanted to escape from— all the insincerity and heartbreak. In a shrill voice she said, "I don't want to talk to you anymore, Mr. Palinski! Will you please leave?"

An older woman, the head of Lisa's department, appeared at her side. "Is there any trouble, Miss Brooks?" she asked smoothly.

Sol gave her an ingratiating grin. "No trouble. Lisa and I just have some business to discuss. How about giving her a little time off?"

Before Lisa could protest, the woman said, "Perhaps that might be better than disrupting the whole department."

Her disapproving glance swept over the knot of sales-girls who were listening avidly. Lisa realized with a sinking heart that her privacy was at an end. She could gladly have strangled Sol Palinski, who was cheerfully impervious to her black scowl.

Giving Lisa's supervisor a little salute, he said, "Thanks, lady, you're a real gent." As they were leaving, he turned back momentarily. "Is one of you gals Shirley Blassick?" Shirley stepped out of the group, a self-conscious look on her face, and Sol extended his hand. "Pleased to meet you," he said.

It was over with in a moment, but not before Lisa saw the bill pass from Sol's hand to Shirley's. The mystery of how he had found her was solved.

Lisa refused to go any farther than the department store cafeteria, a decision Sol mildly agreed to. It soon became obvious, however, that he was going to plead his case vigorously.

"Okay, so you've convinced me that you don't want a career," he said, as soon as they had gotten coffee and were seated at a vinyl-topped table. "But how about the dough? Everybody can use cash."

"I have enough," she replied distantly.

"You mean there's nothing you want to buy?" he persisted. "A mink coat? A flashy car? No place you can think of to put a large chunk of the stuff?"

Lisa became very still. "How much money are you talking about?" she asked cautiously.

"Ahh, that's better." Sol was on firm ground once more. This was what he understood, not all that phony-baloney jazz about not wanting the job.

He mentioned an amount that made her heart beat faster. She could pay Logan back in one lump sum. At what cost though? Could she honestly go back into that life again?

"What would I have to do?" she asked slowly.

Sol's eyes gleamed as he scented victory. "We got this great movie about a woman and a man who—well, you'll read the script for yourself. Just take my word for it, it's fantastic."

"How long would it take?"

"Six weeks, maybe two months tops. But don't get the idea that it's some dog just because we got a tight time schedule." His pride seemed to be at stake. "Longer don't mean better. I got this reputation for bringing things in fast and good, see?"

All of this mattered nothing to Lisa. "So after that I would be through?" she asked.

"Well, other things are bound to turn up," he said, misunderstanding her. "If everything goes like I think it will, you could be a big star."

She shrugged that off impatiently. "I suppose you would want me to sign a contract?"

"Of course, what do you take me for?"

"All right, I'll do it," Lisa said, making up her mind. "But there are to be no options in the contract. A one-picture deal and that's the end of it," she said firmly. Lisa had learned about options by working at Magnum.

He shook his head slowly. "Lady, I don't know if you're a shrewd operator or just plain crazy."

"There is one more thing," she stipulated. "I want an

advance on my salary." She named the amount she owed Logan, expecting a battle from the little producer, yet prepared to stand firm.

He gave in without a murmur, surprising her by taking a checkbook out of his inner pocket and writing her a check on the spot.

The script was delivered by messenger that evening. Lisa curled up on the couch to read it, her casual interest turning to dismay as the plot unfolded. It was the story of a woman hopelessly in love with a man who didn't return that love, but wouldn't allow her to escape. No matter how she struggled against it, his fatal magnetism drew her back time after time, affording him contemptuous amusement.

He wasn't actually like Logan, Lisa assured herself. The man in the script was consciously cruel, while the wounds Logan inflicted were often done unknowingly. The theme of unrequited love was universal too. The trouble was, it hit too close to home.

Lisa sprang to her feet, pacing up and down the small room. What had she let herself in for? Could she go through with it? With a sinking feeling, she realized that she had signed the contract Sol Palinski had the foresight to bring with him. There was little hope that he would let her out of it. Like it or not, she was committed.

Lisa was nervous the first day on the set, especially when she discovered that Rudy Mandell was the cameraman. He was bound to mention to Bruce that she was in this film, something she had hoped to avoid his finding out until after the movie was finished and she had disappeared again.

Lisa no longer harbored any resentment against Bruce. Maybe in his own way he even loved her. Lisa sighed. It didn't really matter. She would just prefer not to see him again.

She wasn't to be that lucky. The second day of shooting, Bruce showed up on the set. Lisa was sitting in a canvas chair going over her lines when he approached her tentatively.

"Lisa?" He was obviously unsure of his reception. "I heard you were back."

She could greet him quite naturally, having been fatalistically prepared for it. "Hello, Bruce, it's nice to see you."

A smile of relief broke out on his face. "Is it? I was hoping you'd feel that way."

She carefully ignored that, remarking impersonally, "You're looking well."

He didn't bother with small talk. "Where have you been, Lisa? I went crazy trying to find you. Why did you drop out without a trace?"

"I felt the need of a change," she said coolly.

"And it's all my fault!" He squatted down in front of her, capturing her unwilling hands. "You don't know how I've cursed myself for that night. You were right, I was drunk—blind, stupid drunk!"

Lisa knew that wasn't true, but there was nothing to be gained by pointing it out. "If you don't mind, Bruce, I'd rather not talk about it."

"Just say you accept my apology and I'll never mention it again."

"All right, I accept your apology."

"And you'll let me see you again?" he asked eagerly.

She finally succeeded in freeing her hands. "I don't think that's a very good idea."

"Which means you don't forgive me," he said flatly.

"It isn't you, Bruce." She sighed. "It's everybody like you—this whole industry. I don't want anything to do with any of you."

"Yet you came back," he pointed out. "Why, Lisa?"

That was something she wasn't prepared to tell anyone. "Only for this one picture. And only because I . . . I needed the money."

"I would have given it to you. I'd give you anything you want," he cried passionately.

She looked into his handsome face, completely un-moved. Why couldn't it be Logan begging her to come back on any terms? But she knew Logan would never beg, even if he wanted her—which he didn't.

"There is nothing you can give me, Bruce," she said sadly.

"Not even love?" he asked softly. When she looked away, he said, "Who is it, Lisa—Logan?"

Her startled eyes flew to his face. "What do you mean?"

"Is he the reason none of us can get to first base with you?"

Lisa's heart was racing, yet she managed to remain outwardly calm. "Where did you get a ridiculous notion like that?"

"You have the look of a woman in love, but not happily. And Logan has a reputation for loving and leaving them. Is that what happened, Lisa? He can be pretty brutal when he has lost interest. Did he tell you it was over? Is that why you ran away?"

"There was nothing to *be* over. Logan and I never had that kind of relationship in spite of what you think. He probably isn't even aware of the fact that I moved."

"Oh, he's aware of it all right. Logan is a cool customer, but he gave me the impression that he was just as frantic to find you as I was."

"You saw him?" Lisa gasped.

"Called him on the phone. Shows you how desperate I was." He gave her a twisted little smile.

"What did he say?" She held her breath.

"About what you'd expect. After he pumped me for all the information I had, he warned me again to stay away from you if you turned up."

"That doesn't prove anything," she said, disappointed. "Logan has never wanted me to associate with movie people."

"Haven't you ever wondered why?"

"He doesn't have any respect for them," she said bluntly. "And he thought I was out of my depth."

"I think it's a lot more than that. I just can't figure it out," Bruce said slowly. "But as long as you don't have any feelings for him, that's all I care about."

"I would prefer not to see Logan again," she said carefully. "Please don't tell him you've talked to me."

"I'm not apt to do that. But he—"

"We're ready for you now, Lisa," the director called.

She rose to her feet. "Good-bye, Bruce."

"Not good-bye." He caught her hands. "I won't accept that."

"They're waiting for me."

"All right," he said, bowing to the inevitable, "but I'll be seeing you."

Lisa's leading man, Rod Selby, didn't look anything like Logan, fortunately. Outside of the fact that he was tall and ruggedly built, the two men couldn't have been more dissimilar. Rod's blond good looks, and the sultry gaze he affected with all his leading ladies, came across potently on the screen, making him a current heartthrob. His conquests in private life were numerous, and he obviously expected to add Lisa to the list.

His appreciative glance took inventory on their first meeting. "If I'd known you were going to be in this flick, I would have worked for nothing," he told her throatily.

"I doubt if that would have pleased your agent," she said tartly.

Undeterred, he cupped her cheek lovingly. "I have a feeling we're going to be great friends before this is over."

Lisa stepped back. "I'd like to save us both some time, Mr. Selby. I'm not interested in any romantic entanglements. That isn't meant as a challenge, nor is it anything personal, I assure you. I would just like to get through this movie as fast as possible with no hurt feelings or temperament delaying the time schedule."

"You really lay it on the line, don't you, lady?" He whistled.

"I thought it was best."

He smiled suddenly, a natural smile, not the carefully

posed one he used on the screen. "Okay, if that's the way you want it. You *will* tell me if you change your mind, though?"

"You'll be the first to know," Lisa assured him, relieved that he was taking it with such good humor.

After that things went smoothly. Rod was of inestimable help, giving her little pointers and never getting impatient if she blew a line. It was all so new to her that she was grateful for his assistance, realizing that he could have made it difficult for her instead.

She had taken Sol Palinski's check to the bank, then written one of her own and mailed it to Logan. He should have received it today, the day Bruce had shown up on the set.

Writing out the check had afforded Lisa a bittersweet satisfaction, putting finis as it did to their relationship. She had meant it when she told Bruce that she didn't want to see Logan again. It would be too painful. With the discharge of her debt, the last tenuous link was broken. She would never see or hear from Logan again.

Chapter Ten

Lisa came to work the next morning completely relaxed, a feeling that wasn't destined to last.

She had been to the wardrobe department where they provided her with a stunning evening gown for the night-club scene that was scheduled. The long, white silk taffeta skirt flowed from a bare-backed bodice completely encrusted with pearls and silver bugle beads, hand-sewn in a swirling design. It felt faintly laughable to be parading around in such elegant finery at eight o'clock in the morning, yet even at that early hour she looked exquisite.

After her hair had been shampooed and curled into a shining nimbus around her head, the makeup man had taken over. Pale green eyeshadow accentuated the emerald sparkle in her eyes, the long thick lashes needing only a touch of mascara. Her full mouth was colored with a hint of pink gloss, the same shade lightly applied to her cheeks. The result was so close to perfection that even the jaded crew accorded her whistles of approbation.

Lisa was smiling when she walked on the set to greet Rod and the director, Tony Blakely. While the lights were being positioned they stood in a little knot, joking about Rod in his tuxedo and Lisa in her evening gown.

"I've come home dressed like this many a morning," he

laughed, "but I've never started out the day in evening clothes."

"I'll bet your eyes are a lot clearer now than they were then," she teased.

Putting his arm around her waist, he jerked her to him, asking with mock severity, "Are you suggesting that I'm a souse, woman?"

The laughing answer she was about to give was stilled on her lips. Over Rod's shoulder as she lifted her face to his, Lisa spied Logan. He was standing just inside the heavy metal door with a warning red light over it that flashed on to indicate the cameras were rolling. From the contemptuous look on his face as he watched her, Lisa knew what interpretation Logan was putting on their innocent byplay. She was transfixed by his mocking eyes, unable to move or speak.

Her sudden tension was transmitted to Rod, who looked at her questioningly. "What's the matter, honey? You're pale as a ghost all of a sudden."

Before she could answer, Logan sauntered over. Both men evidently knew him, and after greetings were exchanged Tony Blakely said, "This is an honor, Logan. Our little production doesn't usually get such august notice."

"I came to talk to Lisa," Logan said. "Will you excuse us?"

The question was a mere formality, understood by both men. Rod and the director withdrew immediately, leaving them alone. Lisa wanted to protest, knowing all the while that it was useless. If Logan wanted to talk to her, that was what he was going to do.

"You're looking well, Lisa," Logan said politely, although his eyes were hard. "It seems I needn't have worried about you after all."

"I didn't know you had," she murmured.

"Oh, yes. But that little disappearing act of yours was cleverly staged, wasn't it?" His mouth curved derisively. "Did you dream it up yourself or did you have help?"

It was what Sol Palinski had accused her of, yet surely

Logan knew her better than that. "How can you ask such a question?" she cried.

"I see. We're going to keep up the fiction, are we?" he asked sardonically.

"What fiction?"

"The charming pretense of the innocent young girl who comes to the big city to get a job as a secretary, having no interest whatsoever in getting into show business."

"It isn't a pretense, it's the truth."

"Amazing! All these good things just happened to you by accident." His voice was heavy with sarcasm.

"I wouldn't exactly call them good things," she said tightly.

"Poor child." His false sympathy was deadly. "Having to endure being in a network television show, and now being forced to star in a movie. All without previous experience too."

Lisa's anger started to rise. "Are you suggesting that I got these parts in the time-honored Hollywood way?"

His face was suddenly grim. "Suppose you tell me."

"Why should I?" she defied him.

His hand shot out and gripped her upper arm painfully. "Because I asked you."

"You won't believe me unless I give the answer you expect to hear!" She tried unsuccessfully to twist away.

"I want the truth, Lisa."

The injustice of his suspicions infuriated her. She had never wanted anything or anybody but Logan. Even now, the remembered feeling of his fingers on her bare skin was doing treacherous things to her self-control. His male magnetism was as potent as ever, drawing Lisa almost irresistibly. After all her good intentions, if he had shown the slightest tenderness she would have launched herself into his arms, no matter what the consequences, no matter what the cost to her self-respect. But Logan hadn't come for that purpose. He had come to hurl insults for her imaginary indiscretions. Well, if that was what he wanted, she would give him reason.

"All right, that's the way it happened. I have a pretty face, as you've been kind enough to point out, and a body that a lot of men seem to want." She threw her head back, facing him with glittering green eyes. "By playing all the angles and using every trick in the book, I've made it to the top."

His hand went to her slim throat. "I could kill you for this," he muttered thickly.

The sharp pain induced by the contempt in his brilliant blue eyes drove her on. "I thought the disappearing act was especially clever. It brought my price up. Men always want what they can't have, don't they?" she taunted.

For a moment Logan's eyes took on a demonic light, his fingers closing in a stranglehold. With great effort he recovered his poise, carefully removing his hand. "I mustn't damage the merchandise," he mocked. "It's your stock in trade, isn't it?"

Despair invaded Lisa's soul. Couldn't he tell she was lying? If he cared anything at all about her, Logan would know that she was incapable of the things she had flung at him. She turned away to hide the tears that threatened, resisting when Logan pulled her back.

"I'm not finished with you yet," he said, distaste coloring his voice.

"I can't imagine what insult you've neglected," she said dully.

"There is the little matter of this check." He thrust it at her.

Lisa recognized her writing. "It's what I owe you," she said tonelessly.

"I don't want it," he bit out.

"Take it, Logan," she begged.

"In spite of your low opinion of me, I don't take money from women."

Her low opinion of him? "I owe it to you. It's money you spent on me."

His eyes were mocking. "I'm used to spending money

on women. Although I must say I usually get more in return."

"I'm sorry I disappointed you in that respect," she said stiffly. "Perhaps this will make up for it."

"You could never make up for the disillusionment, Lisa," he answered softly.

"Logan, I—"

He held up his hand. "Please, no excuses. Enough fiction crosses my desk every day."

"I wasn't going to apologize. What would be the use?" she asked sadly. "Take the check, Logan, I want to be out of your debt."

"And you think this will do it?" His laughter had an unpleasant sound. "I was your sponsor, Lisa, no matter how unwilling. I launched you on your present life of— what would you prefer to call it—success?"

"I would call it purgatory. Take the check, Logan, or this whole exercise has no meaning."

"I don't understand."

"That's the trouble." She sighed. "You never did."

She turned away, but he jerked her back. "You're not going to use me to appease your conscience."

"I have nothing to feel guilty about," she cried, "I consider that the money was a loan. Take it and stop making such a big deal about it."

In answer, he tore the check into tiny pieces, letting them flutter to the floor. "That's what I think of your munificent gesture," he said contemptuously.

"Why did you do that? I'll just send you another one!"

His mouth set in a grim line. "And I'll come back here and do the same thing."

"No, you won't! I'll leave instructions to have you barred from the set."

"Will you now?" he drawled, frosty amusement lighting his eyes.

"Yes, I will! I'm warning you, unless you want to risk embarrassment, don't come around here again."

"So you've gotten big enough to be temperamental. It doesn't take long, does it?" he commented sardonically.

Lisa gritted her teeth. "Think whatever you like. Just don't come back or I'll have you thrown out—bodily if necessary."

"Why don't you start now?" he challenged.

She glared at him, enraged by the derisive look on his face, his whole confident demeanor. "All right, if that's the way you want it." Turning, she searched the set for the director. "Tony, would you come here please," she called.

He approached with a smile on his face. "What can I do for you, honey?"

"I'd like you to ask Mr. Marshall to leave," she said stiffly.

The director looked uncertainly from one to the other. "This is a joke, isn't it?"

"It's no joke," Lisa said hotly. "I don't want him on the set. If he refuses to leave I want you to have him put off."

Logan's broad smile revealed that he was enjoying himself, but Tony looked at her in perplexity. "How could I do a thing like that?"

"For heaven's sake, get a couple of the grips and toss him out," she exclaimed.

"I don't think she understands the problem," Logan said gently.

"You mean she doesn't know this is a Magnum release?" Tony asked.

"What?" Lisa cried. "I don't understand! Sol Palinski said he was an independent producer."

"Lisa, my dear, what a lot you still have to learn about this business," Logan chuckled, his good humor seemingly restored by yet another victory over her. "Where do you think independent producers get their backing? After they put the production together they have to scare up the money to finance it. In this case, Magnum Studios."

"I didn't know," she said hopelessly. "Why didn't Sol tell me?"

Logan shrugged. "He didn't think it would matter." His smile was wolfish. "Only you and I know that it does."

"I . . . uh . . . if you don't need me anymore, there's something I want to check on." Tony wandered away, aware that something was going on that didn't concern him.

"You didn't know I was going to be in this movie, did you?" Lisa asked Logan.

He shook his head. "As I told you, an independent producer is responsible for the complete package—story, cast, crew. Everything except money."

"Which you are supplying," she said dully. When he nodded, she said bitterly, "No wonder you tore up the check. I was trying to pay you off with your own money."

"That had nothing to do with it," he said sharply.

"I'll get out of these clothes and leave," she said quietly.

"Wait a minute." He frowned. "Where do you think you're going?"

"You probably won't believe this, Logan, but I had no idea you were involved in this film. I realize you wouldn't have hired me for the part so I'm saving you the trouble of firing me. Fortunately this is only the third day of shooting. It won't cost much to scrap the footage of me."

"I have no intention of firing you," Logan said coolly. "If Sol thinks you're right for the role, that's good enough for me."

"What if your confidence is misplaced?"

He shrugged. "That's a chance I'll have to take."

"I'll save you the trouble by bowing out now," she said tautly.

He raised a mocking eyebrow. "And let all that scheming and plotting go to waste?"

Lisa's fingernails made little crescent marks in her clenched hands. There was no point in trying to refute his charges; it only gave him an opportunity to wound her further. "I no longer want the part, Logan," she said quietly.

"Why not?" he demanded.

Lisa sighed. "The whole purpose of taking this job was to earn the money to repay you, rather laughable as it turns out. I'll have to find some other way, even if it takes longer."

"Another disappearing act, Lisa?" When she wouldn't look at him, Logan said, "I hate to disappoint you, but whether you like it or not, you're going to show up here every day until this movie is finished."

"Why? You don't want me around any more than I want to be here!"

"Don't be too sure," he said softly. "Maybe I want to see what all the fuss is about. Perhaps I'll stop by every day to check on your progress."

Lisa stared at him in horror, feeling his menacing web entangling her once more. Logan's long-threatened revenge was about to be set in motion. She had a mental picture of what it would be like to have him hovering over her—watching, judging, condemning. He intended to torment her like a sleek jungle cat playing with its prey before destroying it, the poor captive suffering so much in the process that it almost welcomed the coup de grace.

Logan's constant proximity would tear down all the fragile barriers she had tried to erect, and Lisa knew that mustn't be allowed to happen. He must never guess the awesome power he had over her because he wouldn't hesitate to use it. Lisa's body tingled as though he had already begun his practiced seduction.

She drew a shuddering breath. "I'm sorry to spoil your pleasure, Logan, but I'm quitting all the same."

His eyes were enigmatic. "I didn't know you were that wealthy," he said lazily.

"You know I'm not."

"Then where do you expect to get the money to pay the judgment I'll get for breach of contract?"

"You wouldn't sue me," she said uncertainly.

"Wouldn't I?"

If a shark could smile, that's what he would look like, Lisa thought dazedly.

Logan consulted his watch. "I have to get back to the office. I suggest you get on the set. If there is one thing you know about me, Lisa, it's that I expect full value for my money."

She watched his receding back in a kind of numb misery. Once more Logan had come into her life, destroying all her feeble attempts to forget him. This time was the worst, though. There was no longer any pretense that he cared about her. All he wanted now was reprisal.

Lisa got through the day somehow, with a lot of help from Rod.

"Come on relax, baby, you're just walking through your part. What are you doing, saving all your energies for our big love scene tomorrow?" he teased.

"I'm sorry, Rod," she apologized after she had blown her lines for the third time. "I'm just a little upset about something. I'll try to settle down."

"Anything I can to do to help?" he asked sympathetically.

The smile she gave him was twisted. "You're looking at someone who is beyond help, I'm afraid."

Chapter Eleven

The next morning, Lisa was on the set even before her early call. After a restless night, there were dark smudges under her eyes, although it really didn't matter. Tony had elected to do a big love scene this morning, one in which Lisa was supposed to look ravaged because the leading man was leaving her for another woman. In the scene, she would beg him to stay and be devastated by his refusal.

The crew gathered with the usual jokes and easy camaraderie which Lisa found it difficult to join in. She kept looking about nervously for Logan's lean figure and mocking face. The fact that he was nowhere around should have reassured her, yet didn't. He could appear at any time. Logan probably knew she would have this reaction. It was the opening gun in his war of nerves.

For this scene, Lisa wore a satin nightgown covered by a matching pale blue lace and satin peignoir. She had been hesitant about appearing in it even though it wasn't overly revealing. It was the realization of being in a nightgown in front of a lot of men that brought betraying color to her cheeks. Her mental reservation proved to be correct because they teased her unmercifully until Tony brought a halt to it, calling for action.

The scene was Lisa's bedroom. With the ease of a professional, Rod slid smoothly into his role. He was dressed in slacks and an open-neck shirt. As soon as the clack board was snapped, he picked up a tie, sliding it under his collar and buttoning his shirt. There was a hush on the set as the scene began.

"I wish you wouldn't make such a fuss, darling," Rod said. "Didn't we both agree we didn't want any commitments?"

The words had a terrible memory linked to them, but Lisa forced herself into the part of Melanie. "That was in the beginning, Dirk. Before . . . before I fell in love with you."

A look of impatience crossed Rod's handsome face. "You've been in love with a dozen other men."

"I haven't, Dirk! There's been no one but you."

He looked in the mirror, tying his tie. "We've had fun, Melanie, and we'll still see each other now and then if you don't spoil everything by making a scene."

She got up from the bed and crossed to his side, putting her arms around his waist from behind. "I won't make a scene, I promise. Just stay with me tonight—only this one more night."

"What would that prove? It would be the same thing tomorrow night." He tried unsuccessfully to disentangle her clinging arms.

"Why did you have to come back into my life?" she demanded bitterly. "I was just starting to get over you— make a new start. Why couldn't you have left me alone?"

"That's what I'm trying to do," he said cruelly.

"No! I can't go through it again! Don't I mean anything at all to you, Dirk?" she pleaded.

He looked into her exquisite face, passion slowly lighting his eyes. "Of course you do, baby."

He slid his hands inside the peignoir, but instead of melting against him as she was supposed to, Lisa stiffened. Rod leaned forward, and to the camera, it looked as though he was nibbling on her ear. Actually, he whispered, "Relax, honey, it's just playacting."

Lisa forced herself to do as he said, letting him draw her

against his lean body. He was as tall as Logan. Her head rested in the same place on his hard shoulder, her cheek nestling against a muscled chest that seemed hauntingly familiar.

For just an instant, Lisa had the illusion that it was actually Logan holding her near, Logan's arms that were sheltering her as tenderly as they once had. Closing her eyes to capture the illusory moment, she let her hands wander over his broad shoulders.

"I've missed you so," she murmured. When Rod tensed, Lisa twined her arms around his neck. "Don't go. Just hold me like this a little longer."

Rod shook her slightly. "Get ahold of yourself, Melanie," he said meaningfully.

Her startled eyes flew open, meeting the question in his. Then she realized that she hadn't been following the script. Carried away by her intense longing, she had made up her own words of love.

Tears welled up in Lisa's eyes as she stammered, "I . . . I'm sorry."

Rod looked at her warily, which wasn't part of the script, but fit in neatly. The cameras continued to roll as he said, "I'd better go, there's no sense in prolonging this."

"Don't go." She clutched at his arm, the tears overflowing now. "Oh, please don't leave me. What will I do without you?" Melanie's grief, although only part of the play, was very real to Lisa.

Beyond the periphery of blazing lights she could see Tony giving her the thumb and forefinger circle of approval. It made a sob threaten to turn into hysterical laughter. This scene that was too close to reality had penetrated to the very core of longing that filled her days and nights, allowing her misery to spill out for all the world to see. And Tony thought she was acting!

"You'll be fine, Melanie. A smart girl like you will do okay." Rod picked up his jacket and went out the door.

As Lisa watched him go, the camera zoomed in for a closeup of her pain-ravaged face, the wide green eyes shimmering like emeralds in a rippled pond, the long lashes star-pointed by tears. An unreasoning depression settled on Lisa's shoulders as she turned away from the door. *It's only make-believe,* she reminded herself, *a silly pursuit for overgrown children.* But when she threw herself on the bed as the script called for, Lisa sobbed as though her heart would break.

"Cut!" the director called. "Print it. That was great, kids, we got it on the first take."

The punishing klieg lights went off, leaving the set in blessed dimness. Those indispensable men, the grips, bustled around moving furniture, rolling back the monster cameras on their huge, wheeled platforms. A hum of conversation broke out after the enforced quiet, but Lisa didn't move.

She felt drained after the emotional storm she had been through. By dint of great effort she had managed to still the sobs that shook her slender frame; now she was trying to pull herself together in order to face the crew.

A hand closed over her shoulder and a deep voice asked quietly, "Are you all right, Lisa?"

A tremor shook her as she recognized Logan's voice. The bed gave slightly as he sat down on the edge next to her. She remained very still. Strong hands turned her over gently, and Lisa found herself looking into Logan's concerned eyes.

"Are you all right?" he repeated.

Lisa's hands flew up to cover her face. What a mess she must look with the tear stains and her wildly tumbled hair! She didn't want Logan to see her like this. How long had he been here? During the whole scene? The terrible thought made the tears threaten again. Did Logan hear her pleading for love even without commitments? Had he guessed the truth, was that why he was being gentle with her now?

She jumped off the bed, running for her dressing room as though all the Furies were after her.

"Lisa, wait!"

Ignoring Logan's commanding voice, she slammed the door of the trailer assigned to her, leaning against it with bowed head. A knock on the door made her shudder and move to the other side of the room.

"Let me in, I want to talk to you," Logan demanded.

"No! Go away!"

"Stop acting like a child and open this door," he commanded in a gravelly voice.

"We have nothing to talk about and I . . . I'm not dressed."

She could almost see the grim look on his face. "It didn't seem to bother you on the set in front of dozens of other men," he said.

"I . . . that was different. Besides, I was fully covered," she protested. "You're inferring that I was out there half nude."

"I'm telling you that I've seen you in less," he said harshly, "so open this door!"

"Logan! People will hear you."

"It's your choice. If you want everyone in on our private affairs, that's up to you."

Lisa hurriedly unlocked the door, her cheeks flushed. Hastily brushing away the tears, she faced him resentfully. "You always get your own way, don't you? Well, you're here now. What was it you wanted to say?"

He looked at her searchingly, taking in the fevered eyes and uneven breathing. "I was concerned about you, Lisa. I've never seen you like you were out there."

She turned away from his too perceptive gaze, going to the dressing table to pick up a comb. "Surely you've seen performers in action before," she said, trying to control the tremor in her voice.

He came up in back of her, looking at her intently in the mirror. Lisa's heart gave a sudden lurch as every nerve end began to send out signals. The masculine scent of tobacco and aftershave assailed her nostrils, the sight of his rugged face and broad shoulders delighted her eyes, the sound of his deep voice lingered like a siren song in her ears. All of her senses were quiveringly alive to this intensely masculine man whom she loved so much it threatened to destroy her.

"Were you acting, Lisa?" he asked quietly.

Their eyes met and held in the mirror. "What do you mean?" she asked fearfully.

He turned her around, his hands sliding up her neck to cup her head under the tumbled mass of glowing hair. "All that passion, all those tears—were you really just reading words that were written for you?"

So he *had* guessed! Lisa turned her head, her cheek inadvertently nestling into his palm. She closed her eyes, resisting the urge to take the small step that would bring her into his arms.

"Lisa?" His demanding voice broke the spell.

She took a deep breath, lifting her chin. "Are you admitting that maybe I can act after all?"

His narrowed eyes were watchful. "I'm wondering if that's what it was—or if you've gotten in over your head again."

"What are you saying?"

"Is it Rod this time?" His mouth twisted bitterly. "You like blond men, don't you?"

"Is *what* Rod?"

"You must have met him before. Did he get you this job and then something went wrong? Is he tired of you, is that how you could put so much passion into that rejection scene?"

The extent of his misinterpretation made her look at him incredulously. Then, hysterical laughter bubbled up, making it difficult to speak. "You think that Rod and I . . . ? Oh, Logan, how can you be so . . ." Mirthless gales shook her slender body as the tears welled up in her jade green eyes, spilling over onto her pale cheeks.

Logan folded her fiercely in his arms, pressing her head against his shoulder. "It's all right, darling, it's all right," he soothed, stroking her hair.

The familiar smell and feel of him made Lisa cry harder.

Misunderstanding, Logan continued to hold her, murmuring tender words of comfort. When she grew calm he picked her up, carrying her over to the couch where he sat down with her on his lap, rocking her gently like a hurt child. Lisa's arms stole around his neck. Unable to help herself, she buried her face in his throat, shivering with pleasure at the feel of it against her cheek.

His words of comfort were punctuated by light kisses on her temple and eyelids, feathery caresses that lit the flames of desire that were never far away when he was near. Lisa moved closer, feeling his hard chest against her softness. Her hands stole inside his open jacket, tracing the narrowing vee of his splendid torso. Through the silk shirt she could feel his heart racing, and knew he could do the same through her flimsy gown.

Logan drew in his breath sharply, his hands wandering over her back in sudden urgency. Pulling her close, his lips trailed down her cheek, finding her mouth and closing over it with a desperate hunger. There could be no resistance to that fierce male dominance, nor could Lisa have summoned any. With a sigh of pleasure she surrendered, parting her lips to his welcome invasion, holding nothing back, her passion rising to meet his.

Logan's hands caressed her body in a restless exploration, sliding over a silken thigh, a slender waist, moving up to cup a taut breast, as though becoming reacquainted with remembered beauty. His warm mouth touched the hollow in her throat before trailing across her shoulder, pushing aside the strap so his glowing eyes could view the bare satin skin.

Lisa trembled with the need to touch him, slipping her fingers inside his shirt until she could feel the crisp hair that covered his muscled chest. With a groan of pleasure, Logan ripped open his shirt buttons, pulling her gown aside so their bodies met. Moving sensuously against her, he captured her mouth in a long drugging kiss that left her his mindless slave.

"I told you it would be all right, my darling," Logan

murmured, tracing the shape of her ear with his tongue. "You still want me. I can make you forget Rod, little rosebud."

Rod's name provided a jarring note, along with the pet name that Logan had coined for her in Pago Pago. One recalled the painful past, the other the equally painful present. She was in Logan's arms again, but nothing had changed.

Pulling her gown together, Lisa got to her feet before he could stop her. "Still taking care of me, Logan?" she asked, turning her head away.

He cradled her chin in his hand, pulling her gently back to face him. His breathing was ragged, but he managed a lopsided smile. "Somebody has to, and at least I'm used to the job."

"Yes, you've been very good to me. You wouldn't even mind about Rod," she said sadly.

His eyes grew hard. "We won't ever talk about him," he said grimly. "I don't want to hear any details." A look of pain crossed his face so briefly that Lisa realized she must have imagined it. "Just understand that if you come back to me, there won't be any other men."

"You mean I'll be your private property and you'll overlook the fact that I'm slightly damaged," Lisa cried, stung by his suspicions.

His eyes glittered coldly. "That's correct."

"How could you possibly want me under those circumstances?" she marveled.

His mouth tilted in a smile that held no humor. "I believe it's called chemistry. I've wanted you for a long time, Lisa, and as I once told you, I always get what I go after. You have taken longer than usual," he said with calculated cruelty, "but you're going to be mine."

"Still with no commitments I suppose?"

"I believe that's what we agreed on."

She felt like shouting at him, *We didn't agree at all! It's what you want!* But what would be the use?

Lisa turned away wearily. "It's no good, Logan. We

come from different worlds and want different things out of a relationship." To forestall any further objections, she added deliberately, "Besides, it's too late. I've found someone else. I don't want you anymore."

He started toward her menacingly, then checked himself. A dark eyebrow rose mockingly. "Would you like me to refute that one more time?"

"No!" Lisa backed away in alarm.

How many more times could she deny him—and herself? Even now, after he had insulted and degraded her, she wanted him so much that it was a torment to be in the same room with him without being in his arms. Every impulse was urging her to take whatever Logan was willing to give without counting the cost. A businesslike knock on the door brought her back to sanity.

"We're ready for you, Miss Brooks. They're waiting on the set."

Lisa drew a ragged breath. "I have to go."

"Ah yes, your career," Logan said sardonically. "Nothing must get in the way of that, must it?"

When he continued to block the door she slipped past him, being careful that their bodies didn't touch. Logan made no move to stop her, but the contempt in his eyes scourged her like a whip.

Chapter Twelve

The weeks that followed were excruciating torture for Lisa. After their disastrous reunion in her dressing room, Logan stayed away from the set for two weeks. She was just starting to reconcile herself to the idea that he had finally washed his hands of her when he reappeared one day—and irregularly thereafter.

There was no way of predicting when he would show up. Sometimes it was in the morning, at other times in the afternoon, and some days not at all. It made Lisa increasingly jumpy and, inevitably, it began to show in her work. One special day proved to be a disaster. She was so conscious of Logan lurking in the shadows that she blew her lines repeatedly.

Finally Tony called a halt. "What seems to be the trouble, Lisa? Is there something about this scene that bothers you?"

"No, I . . . I'm sorry, Tony. Let's try it again. I'm sure I can get it right this time."

"I think you need a break," he said. "Why don't you go lie down in your dressing room for a while. We'll shoot around you."

"Maybe that would be best," Lisa said gratefully.

Anything to get away from Logan's watchful eyes! Perhaps by the time they were ready for her again he would be gone. It was rather ironic that she had told Rod she wanted to get through this production as fast as possible, and now she was the one who was delaying it.

As Lisa started toward her dressing room, Logan materialized at her side. "What's the matter, Lisa?" he asked silkily. "Is the pressure getting to you?"

She started to tremble. "Why are you doing this, Logan? Why are you trying to sabotage the picture?"

"Would I do that?" he asked mockingly. "After all, I have money involved."

"Then you can see that it isn't in your best interests to keep coming around here."

His eyes were hard. "If you want to be a star, you have to get used to people watching you."

"Watching, yes, but not prejudging," she cried. "Not *hoping* I fail!"

"Is that what you think I'm doing?"

"I know it is! You did everything in your power to keep me out of show business. Now you're even willing to lose money to prove you were right."

"Have you ever thought that maybe I'm doing you a favor? This is the way it is, Lisa. If you didn't have me to contend with, it would be somebody else. This industry isn't for the fainthearted."

"What do you want me to do, admit that you were right, that I hate it?"

"You would have to be a *very* good actress to convince me of that," he said coldly.

She looked at his stern face. The mouth was set in a grim line now, but she knew how it could soften against her own. Lisa's heart turned over. Why couldn't she stop loving him?

"Maybe I'm a better actress than you know," she said bitterly.

A muscle bunched in his jaw. "I faced that fact a long time ago."

"Then leave me alone, Logan!" she cried passionately. "I can't go on with you watching my every move."

"You can't have it all your own way, Lisa," he said softly. His gaze traveled insultingly over her slim body, lingering at the firm breasts and rounded hips. "Getting parts is easy, given your . . . equipment. But you have to perform on the screen as well as off."

Anger swept over Lisa, so intense that it left her shaking. "At least you understand the problem. I much prefer the night work, but I'll see what I can do about my performance in front of the camera."

Logan took a step toward her, then checked himself, clenching his hands. "If you put as much passion into it, who knows what heights you can reach?"

Lisa lifted her chin, her eyes flashing green fire. "I'll try to keep that in mind. Thank you for the suggestion."

She turned to go, but he jerked her back. They glared at each other for a long moment, then Logan's hand went to her face almost unwillingly. A long forefinger traced the delicate high cheekbone that stood out prominently now in her thin face.

"Another suggestion might be that you try sleeping alone a few nights," he said harshly. "Burning the candle at both ends is starting to show on you."

Misery engulfed Lisa. She had to get away before Logan saw how his cruel words wounded her. Pulling away from him, she started for the safety of her dressing room, tears blinding her to the coil of cables on the floor.

"Watch out!" Logan's voice warned.

As her high heel caught in the tangle of thick wires, Lisa pitched forward, clutching at the air. Logan's arms caught her before she fell, gathering her against his hard body. She leaned heavily against him, throwing her arms around his neck to try to regain her balance. Their bodies were molded together for their entire length and Lisa could feel every whipcord muscle in his long frame. Her arms tightened of their own accord and she turned her head blindly, her lips touching the side of his neck.

Logan drew a sharp breath, burying his face in the soft

cloud of her hair for a moment. Then he stood her on her feet, his hands biting into her upper arms. "How many men does it take to keep you happy, Lisa?"

A deep blush colored her pale cheeks. Tearing herself out of his arms, she raced for her dressing room, locking the door behind her. But this time Logan didn't follow.

The long days formed a montage of misery for Lisa, her only consolation being that deliverance would coincide with the end of the picture. She arose at six every morning and worked until late at night, arriving home so blessedly tired that she fell into bed and slept dreamlessly until the next morning when it started all over. She seemed to be living in a vacuum that had no beginning and no end. At least things were running smoothly at the studio, though. By using every ounce of willpower, she managed to perform her role perfectly.

Tony was delighted. "If this part doesn't make you a star, I'll open a shoe store. You're fantastic, Lisa."

"Thank you," she murmured, wondering what he would think if he knew her only motive was to get it over with.

Rod agreed with Tony—with reservations. "You really are great, but you have to learn to pace yourself, honey." He looked at her critically, noting the shadowed green eyes and the slenderness that now bordered on fragility. "You know what all work and no play does to a person. How about having dinner with me tonight?"

"No thanks, Rod. I have to go over my lines for tomorrow."

"That can wait. We'll have an early dinner at Gillio's," he said, mentioning a popular restaurant patronized by show people. "You'll be home in plenty of time to do a quick read-through and still get your beauty sleep."

Lisa was about to refuse again when Tony said, "That's a good idea. We all appreciate your dedication, Lisa, but you are looking kind of finely drawn. A couple of hours off will do you good."

It seemed easier to go than to argue with both of them, so Lisa allowed herself to be persuaded.

"Now aren't you glad you came?" Rod asked when they were seated in a leather booth.

Lisa relaxed against the cushioned back, looking around the crowded, softly lit room. It *was* good to get out for a change. All she had done lately was beat a path from her apartment to the studio and back again. For the first time in ages, she even felt hungry.

"Yes, I'm glad you convinced me." She smiled. "It was nice of you to bother."

"I'm really concerned about you," Rod said with a little frown. "I realize this is your first big part and you want to make good, but you're driving yourself too hard. You're wound up like a tight spring."

"I thought actresses were supposed to be emotional," she said lightly.

"In front of the camera, yes. You have to channel those emotions, though, or you'll burn yourself out and that would be a pity. You're really good, Lisa. I've seen the daily rushes and your performance is stunning. This part was tailor-made for you."

If he only knew! "It would be a tough act to follow," she agreed with a twisted smile.

"Oh, I don't know. I agree with Tony, I think you're going to be a big star. Every bit as big as Monica Miles."

"We're not a bit alike. Why would you think of her?" Lisa asked with distaste.

"Possibly because she's sitting over there with Logan."

Following the direction of his glance, Lisa saw that they were indeed a cozy twosome on the other side of the room. Logan was clasping her hands and talking to her earnestly while Monica watched him with a slight smile on her lovely mouth.

"I wonder if there is anything going on there," Rod mused.

"Can you doubt it?" Lisa asked, carelessly she hoped.

"Oh, I don't mean are they sleeping together. I meant I wonder if she'll manage to lead him to the altar."

Lisa's hands felt icy. "I never thought Logan would marry an actress, but of course she is very beautiful. And if they're in love—" She stopped before her voice broke.

Rod laughed. "You little innocent, what does love have to do with it? Monica would marry him if he had horns and a tail. Do you know what having a husband like Logan could do for her career?"

"But she's already a big star," Lisa protested.

"And not getting any younger," Rod remarked cruelly. "Logan would be a great insurance policy, not to mention the alimony she would get if it didn't work out."

"I think that's rotten!" Lisa cried hotly.

"Don't cry any sad tears for Logan. She hasn't landed him yet," Rod said cynically. "He's a devious dude. To look at him now you would think he was giving her a terrific pitch, but it could be something entirely different. There is one thing you can be sure of, though. Whatever it is *he* wants from *her,* he'll get it sooner or later."

There was no doubt about that, Logan was a winner. But was Rod correct in thinking they only wanted something from each other? Or was he too cynical, too indoctrinated with the Hollywood ethic to recognize real love when he saw it? Lisa could almost hear Logan's low, seductive voice murmuring the tender words that could melt any woman's heart. And Monica's slow smile showed how receptive she was.

Suddenly Lisa wasn't hungry anymore.

Chapter Thirteen

Finally, the movie wound to its inevitable conclusion, and with the end in sight, Lisa felt her leaden spirits rising. There was jubilation on the set when Tony declared it a wrap. An ineffable air of exhilaration pervaded the company, a certainty that they had a hit. At the cast party on the set, everyone was congratulating each other.

"It's a great feeling to know you have a winner," Tony said, his eyes shining.

"How can you be so sure?" Lisa asked. It didn't matter to her personally, yet she would be happy for Tony, and Rod especially.

"It's something you can't explain. After you're in the business for a while you can feel it—you just *know*."

"It helps to have everybody else saying so too," Rod said dryly.

"The picture isn't out yet. How would anyone know anything about it?" Lisa asked.

"This town is almost as bad as Washington when it comes to leaks," Rod laughed. "Every studio in town has their spies in here—or at least a free-lance informant."

Lisa was bewildered. "I don't understand. What difference does it make to them whether the picture is a hit or a flop?"

"You'll find out soon enough." Rod smiled. "When the producers come knocking at your door, trying to outbid each other. Unless I'm sadly mistaken, you're going to be a very hot property in this town."

"I don't believe it," Lisa said flatly.

"Rod is right," Tony told her. "I've heard rumblings already, which doesn't surprise me. The performance you turned in was stunning."

"Thank you," she murmured, embarrassed because only she knew how much of it was acting—and how much wasn't. Logan should get the credit. He was the one who had made her performance credible by forging her in the crucible of pain.

"Don't thank me," Tony said. "I have to admit that when Sol told me he had signed you for the part, I was less than enthusiastic. Nothing personal," Tony added hastily. "It was only because you were an unknown quantity."

"You were right to worry." Lisa smiled. "I had more doubts than you did. I didn't even know what the movie was about until after I signed the contract."

"After this flick is released, you'll be able to pick and choose," Rod assured her. "I wouldn't be surprised if they started approaching you at the party tonight."

She stared at him blankly. "What party?"

"Didn't Tony tell you? Will Westbury is having a party tonight. He's the big banker," Rod explained to Lisa. "His bank is heavily into financing movies."

"I know," she said with reserve.

"You've met him?"

"Once," she answered without elaborating.

"Then you know what his shindigs are like—top drawer all the way. He's having one tonight and we're all invited."

"You can count me out," Lisa said firmly.

"You've got to be kidding! Do you know the kind of people you'll see at one of Westbury's bashes?" Rod asked.

"That's why I'm not going," she answered coolly.

Tony took a hand. "You can't be serious, Lisa. Nobody

turns down an invitation from Wilroy P. Westbury—it's professional suicide. Especially since he mentioned you particularly. You must have made a real impression."

Lisa couldn't have cared less, and told them so. They didn't realize that all their warnings about the detrimental effects on her career fell on deaf ears. She wasn't prepared to disclose the fact that this movie was her swan song in pictures, knowing they wouldn't understand. Only when they explained how it would reflect on them and the film itself did she waver.

"I agree with you that Westbury is an obnoxious little twit," Rod said earnestly, "but he's an influential little twit. When he's displeased, his venom rains down indiscriminately."

"He couldn't blame you for any fancied slight on my part," Lisa protested.

"Oh no? You don't think he would attribute it to his own lack of charm, do you? With his ego, Will would allow himself two choices. Either he would figure that Tony and I conspired to keep you from attending, or he could decide that the atmosphere on the set was so grim that you refused to appear in public with us. Either way, it would start rumors."

"But that's not fair!" she exclaimed.

"I thought you said you had met Westbury," Tony said ironically.

Lisa looked desperately for a loophole, not wanting to hurt these two men who had been so helpful to her, yet unwilling to face another Hollywood party. Especially not one that had such traumatic connotations for her. She clutched at her last straw.

"I don't have anything to wear." It was the classic woman's complaint, but at least in this case it was true.

"Stop by wardrobe and they'll fit you out like a princess," Tony told her.

That was how Lisa found herself that evening, handing her lowly Morris over to a disdainful parking attendant in front of the Westbury mansion. Without explaining the reason to Rod and Tony, the one concession she had insisted on was that she drive herself to the party. In that way she could put in her obligatory appearance and leave as soon as possible.

The young parking attendant's haughtiness vanished as he handed Lisa out of the car. He hadn't expected such elegance to emerge from the lowly conveyance. Her full gold lamé skirt, with matching wide cummerbund, glimmered in the moonlight, the sheer top embroidered with gold and autumn-colored leaves that matched her hair. It was obviously an outfit worth hundreds of dollars. Lisa's eyes sparkled with mischief as she contemplated telling him it was just borrowed finery.

Her mirth faded on entering the elegant house. It might have been an instant replay of last time—the same crowds of sophisticated people in evening clothes, the same music and laughter and high-pitched voices. Lisa forced herself toward the terrace, hoping she could locate Rod and Tony before she ran across her host.

While she was standing self-consciously alone, nerving herself to take the plunge, an older man made his way purposefully toward her.

"I thought you weren't going to show up. You had me worried," he said with a smile.

She looked at him uncertainly. "I'm sorry, do I know you?"

"Not yet, but you're going to," he said confidently. "I'm Myron Stanley of Global Studios."

Before she could comment on this information, they were joined by a heavyset man smoking a fat cigar. "You didn't waste any time did you, Myron?" Without waiting for an answer he turned to Lisa, extending his hand. "Al Glabman, Premier Productions."

"How do you do," Lisa said faintly.

"I hope you haven't been letting Myron razzle-dazzle you," the little fat man said. "He's long on talk, but Premier is where the action is."

"Like that floperoo you had with *Love Is All?*" the first man asked sarcastically. "They had to air out the theater after that bomb."

Nothing they were saying made any sense and she was glad when they were joined by Rod and Tony.

Noting her slightly glazed expression, Rod laughed. "What are you doing to my girl?"

"Just getting acquainted," Myron Stanley said smoothly. "At least that's what I was trying to do when Al horned in."

"Rode to the rescue is more like it," Al said.

"Lisa, darling, how marvelous to see you!" Belva Crystal cried, appearing from nowhere and touching her cheek to Lisa's. "I haven't seen you since that television show we did together. Wasn't it a lark?" Linking arms with her, she turned to the men. "Lisa and I got to be such pals that I couldn't wait to come over and say hello."

Lisa was speechless with amazement, remembering Belva's jealous accusations of scene stealing and her insistence that Lisa be kept as much in the background as possible. Why the sudden show of friendliness? Glancing helplessly at Rod, she noted the derisive twist of his mouth and remembered his prophecy. It seemed he knew what he was talking about. Everyone wanted to climb on her bandwagon—whether they liked her or not. These people, and all they stood for, revolted Lisa.

Searching for a means of escape, she glanced over their shoulders and was horrified to meet Logan's sardonic blue stare. Of course he would be here! She wasn't going to be spared anything. Lisa was sure of it when he approached her group with Monica Miles clinging to his arm.

The newcomers were greeted warmly, with the subtly fawning air accorded to the famous and powerful. For her part, Lisa was silent, but Logan singled her out.

"Congratulations, Lisa, everyone is talking about you." His eyes were enigmatic.

Rod put his arm around her. "Yes, I'm really proud of

my girl." He gave a carefully self-conscious little laugh.
"Although I pride myself that it wasn't all acting in those
love scenes."

Lisa's startled eyes flew to his face. Why was Rod giving
everyone the impression that they were more than just
professionally involved? She struggled out of his embrace,
opening her mouth to issue strong words of protest, which
Rod silenced by covering her mouth with his.

"Play along, baby," he whispered in her ear. "It can't
hurt either one of us."

So Rod was willing to use her too! Before she could
answer, Logan drawled mockingly, "How touching. Do
you two want to be alone?"

Catching the undertone of controlled anger in his voice,
Monica smiled maliciously. "Do you think her other friend
would like that, darling? The one we saw her with at
Rudy's beach house."

"Have you been cheating on me, baby?" Rod asked
Lisa playfully.

Monica looked speculatively at Logan, whose mouth
had thinned to a grim line. "Should I ask you the same
thing—baby?"

Logan's frown was awesome. "I don't—"

As though realizing that she had gone too far, Monica
gave a trill of silvery laughter, linking her arm possessively
through his. "I was only joking, darling. You know I trust
you implicitly."

Lisa's heart plunged at this confirmation of what she had
seen in the restaurant. Monica was Logan's real love. Was
he angry that she doubted it?

"Are congratulations in order, or is it a case of wishful
thinking?" Rod asked Monica sardonically, his eyes on
Logan's stormy face.

The glare Monica sent Rod was filled with venom,
although she tried to cover it with a dazzling smile. "If you
were a woman, darling, that would be considered a catty
remark. I do think it's so sad when a man has trouble with

his own love life. It makes him slightly bitter. Especially when he's a so-called sex symbol."

"Anyone who isn't sure of the target gets tense." Rod grinned. "We so-called sex symbols are an insecure lot, aren't we, Monica?"

The undercurrents of intrigue and backbiting were making Lisa feel actually ill. She had to get away from these dreadful people before they finished rending each other and turned on her once more.

Lisa was starting to edge away when Logan's frowning voice stopped her. "Where are you going?"

She fumbled in her evening purse, saying vaguely, "Excuse me, I . . . I seem to have forgotten something." Turning back toward the house, she fled rapidly down the wide hall and out the front door.

It seemed like forever until her car was produced. Lisa was sure that someone would come out to try to prevent her leaving, but they had evidently accepted her ambiguous excuse as meaning that she wanted to visit the powder room. Finally the little Morris appeared. Breathing a sigh of relief, Lisa got in hurriedly and gunned it down the driveway.

Misery was her companion on the ride home. She never should have allowed Rod and Tony to talk her into coming. Why didn't she realize that Monica and Logan would be there? Just seeing them together was like a knife in her midsection. Monica's confirmation of their relationship wasn't unexpected, but it hurt all the same.

And all those terrible people—the two movie moguls trying to one-up each other, Belva with her insincere praise, and even Rod whom she had trusted, turning out to be like all the others, wanting to cash in if possible on her success. His actions must really have crystallized Logan's suspicions of her. That withering look was the crowning blow.

Well, it didn't matter anymore, she was free of all of them. A resigned sort of calm descended on Lisa as she made her plans. There was nothing to keep her in Los Angeles any longer. It had been a mistake to come here in the first place. She would go back to Abilene where she should have stayed after the death of her father. All she had succeeded in doing was exchanging one kind of heartbreak for another.

Back at her apartment, Lisa took off her gown and hung it on its padded hanger. It would go back to the studio tomorrow. Next, she put on a short ruffled cotton housecoat and took her suitcase down from the top shelf of the bedroom closet. Every movement was deliberate, as though the task before her required the utmost concentration. Only in this manner could she control the emotions that seethed just under the surface, waiting to destroy her if she faced the wasteland her life had become.

Stockings and panties went on the bottom of the case, to be followed by blouses neatly folded. Lisa's mind was carefully blank as she selected the dresses that would go in next. She was so withdrawn that the doorbell rang a second time before it registered.

Then her heart started to pound. With a dull certainty, she knew it was Logan. Maybe if she remained very still he would think she wasn't home. Even as the futile thought occurred, she rejected it. Her car was outside and that repeated pounding didn't sound like he was going to give up. She had better let him in before he woke the neighborhood. What difference did it make anyway? She might as well tie up this last loose end, say good-bye and get him out of her system for all time.

Opening the door, Lisa sought to postpone the recriminations. "How did you find me?" she asked.

Logan sauntered into the small living room, insolently eyeing her slender body in the thin cotton robe. When she flushed and pulled it closer around her slim figure, his mocking smile deepened.

"My dear Lisa, I could have come here any time I wanted. Your vital statistics are a matter of record at the studio."

"Which you own," she said tonelessly.

"That's close enough," he agreed.

"What do you want?" she asked bluntly.

"You mean it's mine for the asking?" One dark eyebrow peaked sardonically. "No more coy little games?"

He leaned against the couch, hands in the pockets of his trousers. It tightened the fabric over his muscular thighs, outlining their powerful length. Lisa turned her eyes away, a lump rising in her throat. In the elegant black and white evening clothes, he was impossibly handsome—and remote. How had they reached this impasse? Where was the man who used to treat her like someone special? Logan could barely be civil to her now. Whatever he felt for her was dead. The mockery in those blue eyes that had once flamed with such passion was suddenly more than Lisa could endure.

"I'm tired, Logan. Couldn't you leave me alone just this one night?" she begged.

He came over to stand uncomfortably close to her. "That has a very erotic sound, my dear."

"You know what I mean."

When she would have moved away, he caught her wrist, preventing it. "Did you get a better offer tonight? It wasn't very good business on your part to run away like that without hearing mine."

She masked the hurt his words inflicted. "Would you really join those other men in bidding for me?"

Something flamed briefly in his eyes, then was deliberately hidden. "Why not? By now you represent a challenge."

"One you would tire of as soon as you bested it," she said bitterly. "I'm actually doing you a favor by not giving in."

His long fingers found the nape of her neck underneath the shining hair, sensuously stroking the sensitive skin. "But aren't you penalizing yourself?" he asked softly.

Startled green eyes flew to his face. "What do you mean?" she whispered.

"I haven't told you what I'm prepared to do for you."

Relief that he hadn't discovered her secret was mitigated by rising anger. "I believe I already know."

"Shame on you, Lisa." The smile he gave her was almost natural. "I was referring to the furtherance of your career."

"Oh, that again," she intoned wearily.

A thoughtful frown puckered his forehead. "You're a surprisingly good actress for having no experience. Of course there are a lot of rough edges, but that's easily taken care of. What I propose is sending you to drama school."

She looked at him in amazement. "I thought you didn't want me to be an actress."

"I don't, but if you have your heart set on it, at least I want you to be a good one."

"Those people tonight seemed to think I already am."

Logan's mouth thinned to a grim line. "Those people tonight want to send you up like a skyrocket so that they can benefit by your light. They don't care that you'll come down just as fast."

He was right of course. If she truly was as good in this picture as they said, it was only because she was acting out her own life. Lisa was too intelligent not to realize that.

"I don't want to go to drama school, Logan," she said in a low voice.

He took her chin in his thumb and forefinger, forcing it up brutally. His eyes blazed with a brilliant blue light. "I won't let you destroy yourself because those stars in your eyes are blinding you to reality. If you let them use you, you'll wind up a disillusioned has-been in six months."

"Why do you care, Logan?" she asked hopelessly. "If I ended up on the cutting room floor at least one of us would be happy."

He stared at her for a moment in suppressed fury. Then his hands threaded through her hair, pulling her head back sharply. All of his pent-up rage exploded in a kiss so punishingly savage that she could hardly breathe. When his teeth pressed painfully into her lower lip, Lisa gave a whimper of protest.

The small sound registered and he eased the pressure, his mouth moving on hers with seduction now. The slow, sensuous exploration gained him the entry he wanted as her lips parted helplessly to his invasion.

Logan's hands hastened the victory, sliding down to her hips and pulling her against his demanding body. Lisa started to tremble as her aroused senses flamed to joyous life. This was what she had longed for every solitary, lonely night, to melt against him and reassure herself of his desire. The fact that it was the last time he would ever hold her like this made the moment even more poignant. Her arms went around his neck and she clasped her hands in back of his head, holding him to her while she said a silent good-bye.

Logan's breathing was ragged as he lifted his head to stare at her. Then his mouth twisted bitterly. "It looks like we've made a deal. I'll do something for you . . . and you'll do something for me."

For a moment Lisa didn't think she had heard correctly. "You said I'd never have to make a trade," she said in an agonized whisper.

The eyes Logan turned on her were hard. "I'm a man, Lisa, and I want you. I'm tired of waiting while you turn to other men to fulfill your consuming ambition. It goes against every one of my principles, but if that's the only way I can get you, I'll make you a star."

A shudder went through Lisa's slight frame. There was no passion on Logan's face now, only grim determination. She was just a commodity to be bought and used and cast aside after a while. A sob rose in her throat, but she held it back. Commodities don't cry, she thought wildly, turning and running into the bedroom.

Logan followed her before she could slam the door. "You aren't getting away this time. I told you I—" The words broke off as he saw the open suitcase on the bed. "What's that for?" he asked, frowning.

"I'm going back to Abilene," she said tonelessly. It didn't matter now if he knew.

"For a visit you mean?"

"No, for good."

"I don't understand. Why?"

She gave a sad little smile. "You've just answered your own question. It's because you *don't* understand, Logan. You never did."

He searched her face intently. "What are you trying to say, Lisa?"

"You never trusted me, Logan. You were always searching for signs that I was like all the others, out to get something from you. It was almost as though you were relieved when you found indications that seemed to be pointing that way." He started to speak, but she rushed on. "The men that you accused me of sleeping with to get ahead. None of it was true. And that career you accused me of scheming for—I didn't want it."

His expression was unreadable. "You left me for a job in television."

"Only because I was angry at the rumors people were spreading about us, and your part in starting them. I went to Bruce for a secretarial job and he offered me a part instead. I only took it because I needed the money to live on. I agreed to the movie job because it gave me enough money to repay you." She looked at him piteously. "But even that didn't work out."

"If all of this is true, it still doesn't explain why you tried to drop out of my life completely. Didn't our friendship mean anything to you?"

"We haven't been friends for a long time, Logan," she said sadly. "Actually, I don't suppose we ever were. Can you honestly say that what you felt for me was friendship?"

His eyes wandered over her delicate face and enticing body, darkening with an emotion that Lisa was too distraught to recognize. "No, I guess not."

"I forced my way into your life like an injured bird flying through an open window. You felt sorry for me so you fed me and took care of me," she said. "But that wasn't friendship, it was just a sense of responsibility. Well, I didn't want you to feel responsible anymore and that's why I went away."

"Was it, Lisa?" he asked softly. "Be honest with me. Wasn't it because of the way I tried to make love to you when I brought you home from Westbury's party?"

She looked away from him, not wanting to relive that terrible night. "Perhaps that had something to do with it," she admitted faintly.

He took her chin in his hand, turning her gently back to face him. "You don't know how I've hated myself for that. I was the one who wanted to protect you and, ultimately, I was the one you had to be afraid of."

His eyes were tortured and Lisa said quickly, "No, Logan, I was never afraid of you."

His remorse had to be expressed. "What can I say in my own defense? That I was feeling murderous at the thought of Bruce touching you? That I wanted to beat up on every man at the party who even looked at you?" His fingers combed restlessly through her silken hair as he devoured her with his eyes. "You don't belong in this business. You shouldn't be around any of us."

The thought that Logan still cared enough to protect her was somehow comforting even though it wasn't what she yearned for. At least it was something to take away with her. She sighed deeply. "You're right, Logan, I don't belong here. That's why I'm going home."

"No! Don't go, Lisa." He took her cold hands in his. "Stay here and let's try to start over. I promise that things will be different. I'll make it up to you, I swear!"

"I wish you didn't feel so guilty, Logan." She gave him a woebegone little smile. "In spite of all your fears, I survived intact."

"You mean you got over Bruce," he said flatly.

"There was nothing to get over. I was never in love with Bruce, he was just a good friend." She looked away uncomfortably. "At least I thought he was. I guess I'm pretty stupid about men."

"Or perhaps you don't know what effect you have on them," Logan said grimly. "How about Rod? Are you telling me he left you unscathed? He seemed pretty anxious to inform one and all that you were more than just friends."

"You should have been able to see through that little performance, even though it came as a surprise to me," she said bitterly. "I wouldn't have either one of them as a consolation prize."

Logan's eyes narrowed, becoming suddenly intent. "If it isn't Bruce or Rod, who are you running away from?"

"I . . . I'm not running away from anyone."

"It isn't because you're in love with someone and it didn't work out?" he persisted.

Lisa's long eyelashes fluttered down to touch her flushed cheeks. "No," she murmured.

"Don't lie to me, Lisa!" He forced her chin up, glaring at her. "Who is he? Where did you meet him?"

His taut body was just inches from her own and Lisa wanted so desperately to close the gap that it made her knees feel weak. She couldn't look at him, afraid that her expression might reveal her secret. When he wouldn't release her chin she said, "You have no right to ask me that. I didn't ask you about Monica, did I?"

"What does she have to do with us?" Logan frowned. "I don't want to talk about Monica."

Lisa's degradation was complete. He didn't want to discuss the woman he loved with the one he had merely wanted to bed down.

"Don't worry, I wasn't trying to find out the date so I could leak it to the gossip columns," she said bitterly.

Logan ran distracted fingers through his hair. "Date? What date?"

Lisa's shoulders slumped and she turned away from him. "All right, if that's the way you want it."

He turned her back to face him. "I honestly don't know what you're talking about, but I gather you think there is something going on between Monica and me."

"Why bother to deny it to *me?* You haven't exactly tried to hide it from the rest of the town," she said resentfully. "You're always together—at Rudy Mandell's, at Will Westbury's parties."

"Always at parties," Logan said softly. "Doesn't that tell you something, Lisa?"

"Not always!" she flared. "How about the night at Gillio's? There were only the two of you then."

Logan looked puzzled. "How do you know about that?"

"I was there. I saw you. You were holding hands and whispering very interesting things in her ear, judging by her expression." Lisa's throat felt suddenly constricted. "Is that the night you got engaged?"

Something blazed in Logan's eyes, turning them as brilliant as sapphires. His hands moved caressingly on her shoulders. "Would it make a difference? Would you mind if I married Monica?"

It was on the tip of Lisa's tongue to shout that she couldn't care less who he married, but the words wouldn't come out. When you love someone, you don't want him to be hurt. Monica was the type of female who was incapable of loving anyone except herself, yet how did you tell a man that the woman he intended to marry wasn't good enough for him?

"I want you to be happy, Logan," she said carefully. "I don't think you should rush into marriage."

"Don't you, my sweet?" he murmured, trailing his fingertips down her cheek. "I'm sorry to hear that because I've been giving the matter an awful lot of thought lately."

Lisa's heart sank. It was bad enough to have to give him up, but not to a woman like that. "She's all wrong for you," she cried, throwing caution to the winds. "She only wants what she can get out of you! Can't you see? She is everything you told me you despise in these people."

"You're so right." He smiled, tracing the shape of her trembling mouth.

"But if you *know* that, how can you possibly think of marrying her?"

"I never have," he said calmly. "To be brutally frank, I can't stand the woman."

Lisa looked at him helplessly. "I don't understand."

"That's what you accused me of earlier and I'm beginning to think that we're both guilty." He put his arms around her waist, watching her closely as he said, "If you don't care about me, Lisa, if all you want to do is put as much distance between us as possible, why do you care if I botch up my life?"

She bent her head, carefully twisting one of his shirt buttons in her shaking fingers. "I . . . I do care about what happens to you, Logan."

"After all the rotten things I've done to you?"

"You don't stop loving someone just because—" Lisa's head shot up, her eyes wide with horror at the inadvertent admission.

Logan's face went very white under his tan. He stared at her wordlessly before sudden joy flamed on his face. Folding her in his arms, he crushed her so tightly that her fragile bones were in danger. "Oh, my darling! Do you really mean it? I never guessed!"

For just a moment Lisa allowed herself the ecstasy of being in his arms. Her hands wandered restlessly over his back, touching the bunched muscles, tracing the width of his broad shoulders. Then sanity returned and she pulled away.

"You don't have to feel sorry for me," she said in a small voice.

He framed her face in his palms, looking at her with eyes that were darkened almost to navy. "Is that what you think I feel?"

"I'm glad you never guessed," she whispered. "I tried so hard to keep it from you."

"You'll never know how well you succeeded," he groaned. "There were times when I thought you hated me."

"Oh no, Logan, you couldn't have thought that!" Her cheeks bloomed with color. "You're much too experienced not to know how you affected me."

He stroked her hot cheek tenderly. "Yes, my darling, I knew how to play on your beautiful body until you wanted me, but I thought it was because you were so innocent. That any accomplished lover could do the same. It drove me wild to think that Bruce—"

She put her fingers over his mouth to stop the tortured words. "There was never anyone but you."

"Then why wouldn't you let me make love to you?"

This was the hard part. Could she make him understand when sometimes it had been difficult to convince herself that she was doing the right thing? "I knew you wanted me, Logan," she began in a low voice. "But it wasn't the way I wanted you. I was only a challenge to you, someone you would tire of in a short while. I wanted to be more than just another body slipping briefly through your bed."

He looked at her incredulously. "You mean you couldn't tell that I'm crazy, out of my mind in love with you?"

Lisa almost stopped breathing. "You . . . you love me?"

The smoldering passion in his eyes threatened to break into flames. "Would you like me to show you how much?"

Lisa looked at him in a daze. "But you and Monica—"

An expression of disgust crossed his face. "It's time to clear that up and then I don't want to hear her name again. As I told you in the beginning, there are certain things in this business that are distasteful, but necessary. Our big picture for next year is going to be the life of Mata Hari. It has everything—sex, suspense, intrigue. Monica is perfect for the part. In spite of being a rotten person, she's a good actress, but she's playing hard to get. I've been romancing her in an effort to get her to sign."

Lisa's jealousy was immediate and consuming. The thought of them together was almost more than she could bear. "I think that's disgusting!" she cried indignantly. "How could you do such a thing when you were the one who was so contemptuous of people who sold their bodies to get what they wanted."

Surprisingly, Logan laughed. "My sweet little rosebud, I keep forgetting that you're new to the business. The term 'romancing' isn't what you think. I mean I've been taking her to all the right places and dancing attendance on her, paying her extravagant compliments. But that's *all* I've done. I wouldn't sleep with that woman for this movie or any other," he said bluntly. "As a matter of fact, if she doesn't sign soon, I'm going to dump her. She isn't the only one who can do the part."

Lisa was like a sleepwalker waking from a long nightmare. Out of all the chaotic events that had occurred, one thing stood out like a gift from heaven—Logan said he loved her!

"I didn't realize," she faltered.

"Well, now you do." He smiled.

Logan swept the open suitcase onto the floor, heedless of the contents that jumbled together in a tangled mass. Swinging Lisa into his arms, he lowered her to the bed, lying next to her and straining her against his lean body.

"We've put each other through hell, but at least it's over," he said, his mouth warm against the pulse that beat wildly in her throat. "Let me love you, Lisa," he groaned. "No commitments, just love me."

His words sliced through her painfully, but she knew that this man was her destiny. If all she could have was a tiny part of him, then that was how it would have to be, because without him she was only half alive.

"If that's the way you want it, Logan," she sighed, winding her arms around his neck and capitulating.

"It isn't what I want, darling," he murmured against her satin skin. "But I'm willing to take anything you'll give me."

His hands were building fires in her body that threatened to burn out of control, yet Lisa's dazzled mind managed to register his regretful words. "What do you mean?" she gasped, stilling the hand that was caressing her breast.

"What I really want is to marry you, sweetheart. I want my ring on your finger to proclaim to the whole world that you belong to me forever."

"But all this time—as far back as Pago Pago on the yacht, you assured me that if I came to you, it would be without commitments."

He kissed her gently. "You had made your views on the subject very clear and I was afraid I'd frighten you off if you knew how I really felt, so I pretended I didn't want any ties either. I can't pretend any longer, but it's all right, darling. It's enough to know that we belong to each other. A piece of paper couldn't make me love you any more. Nothing could."

Unexpected tears spilled over at his tenderness, and Logan kissed them away. "Don't cry, angel, I promise I'll never try to pressure you into anything you don't want."

She gave him a watery smile. "If you're not doing anything tomorrow, Logan, do you think you could find time to marry me?"

Incredulous joy flamed in his eyes as he cupped her face in his palms. "Do you really mean that, Lisa?"

Her long eyelashes fell as she untied his tie. "Unless that's too long to wait."

A long time later, he stirred in her arms. His lips slid warmly over her bare shoulder. "I have a confession to make. I lied to you, rosebud." She looked at him uncertainly and was reassured by the teasing light in his eyes. "I intended all along to trick you into marriage."

"How?"

"I felt sure you would want our baby to have a father," he said mischievously.

"Now why didn't I think of that?" Lisa marveled as Logan reached for her again.

IT'S YOUR OWN SPECIAL TIME

Contemporary romances for today's women.
Each month, six very special love stories will be yours
from SILHOUETTE. Look for them wherever books are sold
or order now from the coupon below

$1.50 each

☐ 5 Goforth	☐ 28 Hampson	☐ 54 Beckman	☐ 83 Halston
☐ 6 Stanford	☐ 29 Wildman	☐ 55 LaDame	☐ 84 Vitek
☐ 7 Lewis	☐ 30 Dixon	☐ 56 Trent	☐ 85 John
☐ 8 Beckman	☐ 32 Michaels	☐ 57 John	☐ 86 Adams
☐ 9 Wilson	☐ 33 Vitek	☐ 58 Stanford	☐ 87 Michaels
☐ 10 Caine	☐ 34 John	☐ 59 Vernon	☐ 88 Stanford
☐ 11 Vernon	☐ 35 Stanford	☐ 60 Hill	☐ 89 James
☐ 17 John	☐ 38 Browning	☐ 61 Michaels	☐ 90 Major
☐ 19 Thornton	☐ 39 Sinclair	☐ 62 Halston	☐ 92 McKay
☐ 20 Fulford	☐ 46 Stanford	☐ 63 Brent	☐ 93 Browning
☐ 22 Stephens	☐ 47 Vitek	☐ 71 Ripy	☐ 94 Hampson
☐ 23 Edwards	☐ 48 Wildman	☐ 73 Browning	☐ 95 Wisdom
☐ 24 Healy	☐ 49 Wisdom	☐ 76 Hardy	☐ 96 Beckman
☐ 25 Stanford	☐ 50 Scott	☐ 78 Oliver	☐ 97 Clay
☐ 26 Hastings	☐ 52 Hampson	☐ 81 Roberts	☐ 98 St. George
☐ 27 Hampson	☐ 53 Browning	☐ 82 Dailey	☐ 99 Camp

$1.75 each

☐ 100 Stanford	☐ 114 Michaels	☐ 128 Hampson	☐ 143 Roberts
☐ 101 Hardy	☐ 115 John	☐ 129 Converse	☐ 144 Goforth
☐ 102 Hastings	☐ 116 Lindley	☐ 130 Hardy	☐ 145 Hope
☐ 103 Cork	☐ 117 Scott	☐ 131 Stanford	☐ 146 Michaels
☐ 104 Vitek	☐ 118 Dailey	☐ 132 Wisdom	☐ 147 Hampson
☐ 105 Eden	☐ 119 Hampson	☐ 133 Rowe	☐ 148 Cork
☐ 106 Dailey	☐ 120 Carroll	☐ 134 Charles	☐ 149 Saunders
☐ 107 Bright	☐ 121 Langan	☐ 135 Logan	☐ 150 Major
☐ 108 Hampson	☐ 122 Scofield	☐ 136 Hampson	☐ 151 Hampson
☐ 109 Vernon	☐ 123 Sinclair	☐ 137 Hunter	☐ 152 Halston
☐ 110 Trent	☐ 124 Beckman	☐ 138 Wilson	☐ 153 Dailey
☐ 111 South	☐ 125 Bright	☐ 139 Vitek	☐ 154 Beckman
☐ 112 Stanford	☐ 126 St. George	☐ 140 Erskine	☐ 155 Hampson
☐ 113 Browning	☐ 127 Roberts	☐ 142 Browning	☐ 156 Sawyer

$1.75 each

- [ ] 157 Vitek
- [ ] 158 Reynolds
- [ ] 159 Tracy
- [ ] 160 Hampson
- [ ] 161 Trent
- [ ] 162 Ashby
- [ ] 163 Roberts
- [ ] 164 Browning
- [ ] 165 Young
- [ ] 166 Wisdom
- [ ] 167 Hunter
- [ ] 168 Carr
- [ ] 169 Scott

- [ ] 170 Ripy
- [ ] 171 Hill
- [ ] 172 Browning
- [ ] 173 Camp
- [ ] 174 Sinclair
- [ ] 175 Jarrett
- [ ] 176 Vitek
- [ ] 177 Dailey
- [ ] 178 Hampson
- [ ] 179 Beckman
- [ ] 180 Roberts
- [ ] 181 Terrill
- [ ] 182 Clay

- [ ] 183 Stanley
- [ ] 184 Hardy
- [ ] 185 Hampson
- [ ] 186 Howard
- [ ] 187 Scott
- [ ] 188 Cork
- [ ] 189 Stephens
- [ ] 190 Hampson
- [ ] 191 Browning
- [ ] 192 John
- [ ] 193 Trent
- [ ] 194 Barry
- [ ] 195 Dailey

- [ ] 196 Hampson
- [ ] 197 Summers
- [ ] 198 Hunter
- [ ] 199 Roberts
- [ ] 200 Lloyd
- [ ] 201 Starr
- [ ] 202 Hampson
- [ ] 203 Browning
- [ ] 204 Carroll
- [ ] 205 Maxam
- [ ] 206 Manning
- [ ] 207 Windham

$1.95 each

- [ ] 208 Halston
- [ ] 209 LaDame
- [ ] 210 Eden
- [ ] 211 Walters
- [ ] 212 Young
- [ ] 213 Dailey
- [ ] 214 Hampson
- [ ] 215 Roberts
- [ ] 216 Saunders

- [ ] 217 Vitek
- [ ] 218 Hunter
- [ ] 219 Cork
- [ ] 220 Hampson
- [ ] 221 Browning
- [ ] 222 Carroll
- [ ] 223 Summers
- [ ] 224 Langan
- [ ] 225 St. George

- [ ] 226 Hampson
- [ ] 227 Beckman
- [ ] 228 King
- [ ] 229 Thornton
- [ ] 230 Stevens
- [ ] 231 Dailey
- [ ] 232 Hampson
- [ ] 233 Vernon
- [ ] 234 Smith

- [ ] 235 James
- [ ] 236 Maxam
- [ ] 237 Wilson
- [ ] 238 Cork
- [ ] 239 McKay
- [ ] 240 Hunter
- [ ] 241 Wisdom
- [ ] 242 Brooke
- [ ] 243 Saunders

—#244 STARS IN HER EYES, Sinclair
—#245 STEAL LOVE AWAY, Trent
—#246 WHERE TOMORROW WAITS, Carroll
—#247 MOUNTAIN MELODY, Halldorson
—#248 ROSE-COLORED GLASS, St. George
—#249 SILVERWOOD, Scofield

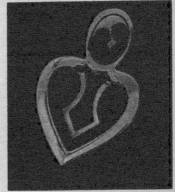